SHOOTOUT AT SIOUX WELLS

The herd had trailed 1,000 miles from Texas and had survived parched-dry land and forded dangerous rivers. They'd come through storm and lightning; two men died in the mission. But nothing prepared them for the wild stampede when the cattle refused to cross the strange new tracks and the engineer cut loose his whistle. The result was disaster for Zack Keech and his father Brandy Ben.

Later Zack found himself working as an undercover agent for two odd railroad owners and notorious Wild Bill Hickok himself. The action entangled cattlemen, railroaders, a pretty black-eyed vixen, and a mule-stubborn trail driver, all surrounded by gunfire and the threat of sudden death . . .

CANCELLED

SHOOTOUT AT SIOUX WELLS

Cliff Farrell

GLADSTONE
CITY
LIBRARY

GUNSMOKE

This hardback edition 2005
by BBC Audiobooks Ltd
by arrangement with
Golden West Literary Agency

Copyright © 1973 by Cliff Farrell.
All rights reserved.

ISBN 1 4056 8051 2

British Library Cataloguing in Publication Data available.

Printed and bound in Great Britain by
Antony Rowe Ltd., Chippenham, Wiltshire

Shoot-out
at Sioux Wells

Chapter 1

Brandy Ben Keech, owner and trail boss of the K-Bar-K herd, slid from his horse, removed his hat and hurled it on the ground. The hat was hand-made of brushed beaver and had cost him thirty dollars in San Antonio. It had suffered considerably from wear and weather, and now Brandy Ben leaped high in the air, and landed on it with spurred boots, completing its destruction.

"Drat the danged, double-dratted, pig-headed, triple-cussed sons of Satan!" he screeched. "Dang all cow cattle to condemnation! Drat! Drat! Drat!"

Some months previously Brandy Ben had taken a solemn vow to his wife and to their community preacher at the little cow-town church in the Brazos country that he would forgo the use of strong language and would never again take the Lord's name in vain. Therefore, he was somewhat handicapped in attempting to express his feelings.

Along with the K-Bar-K crew, he had trailed the herd nearly a thousand miles up the country from deep in Texas, enduring his share of the customary miseries that go with handling three thousand head of wild Longhorns. He and his riders had survived dry drives and the crossing of such items as the Red River and the Arkansas. They'd had their stampedes on nights of storm and lightning. They had lost two men, one from natural causes— a broken leg when a horse fell, and the other still lingering in the Dodge City jail after an attempt to run Marshal Wyatt Earp and the town up a tree.

7

Now they were in the short-grass country of the plains, and they could not force the cattle to cross a measly railroad track that had cropped up unexpectedly, blocking their route. The track stretched across the swells as far as the eye could carry into the plains.

The cattle had never before seen a railroad track, and it was the nature of the Longhorn to be wary of objects that were not within its past experience. Brandy Ben had been lucky when the herd had approached the Santa Fe Railway right-of-way near Dodge two weeks in the past. A cloudburst had washed out a long section of track, through which the Longhorns had passed peaceably.

When a Longhorn made up its mind to be obstinate, it was obstinate indeed. In this case, its strength was three-thousand-fold. Brandy Ben and the crew had been trying for three hours to induce the mass of perversity to cross that narrow stretch of imaginary danger. They had coaxed, wheedled, threatened and prodded. The only result was a growing spirit of rebellion among the cattle. The animals were on the knife-edge of stampeding.

Brandy Ben's son rode up and dismounted beside his enraged father. "Easy, easy!" he said. "Quit dancing around like a drunk yahoo. You'll start the herd running. We don't want that to happen, and 'specially not here. We'd lose a lot of them if they headed into that stuff to the south."

Brandy Ben's jowls swelled and became crimson under his stubble of wiry, graying beard. He wasn't in the habit of taking advice from anyone, least of all his son. It graveled him that he had to look up into his son's face. Zack Keech was an inch past six feet, and Brandy Bill fell five inches short of that height, much to his secret chagrin.

"What in Tophet do you say we do, if you're so danged smart?" he demanded. "Maybe you figure we ought to stay here 'til we decide they won't be et up by that railroad track? An' where did that blasted thing come from anyway? Nobody told me there was a railroad across this stretch of country."

Zack looked around. His father did not make many mistakes in rodding a trail herd, but he had made one this time. He had failed to have the route scouted ahead, taking it for granted that the going would be easy across open plains for the next hundred miles or more. But the herd was milling uneasily in a cul-de-sac, with the railroad track blocking the way north, and a maze of coulees and alkali marshes stretching to the east and south. The only path was the area over which the cattle had traveled into this unexpected blockade, and it would take time and patience to induce them to return over grass they had so recently trampled.

Bib Olsen joined them. "I've heard that Shanghai Pierce had a herd that wouldn't cross the U.P. tracks up Julesburg way a year or two back," he said. "Shanghai an' his crew built a sod an' dirt path across the tracks, an'—"

"Yeah!" Brandy Ben raged. "An' it took them days of hard work. They sent into town for shovels an' such. All we've got is the wagon shovel an' a pick with a busted handle. Maybe I haven't told you, Bib Olsen, that I've got a contract to deliver these jugheads to the Crow agency on the Missouri River by the middle of September, with a penalty of one hundred dollars a day for every day I'm late. It's well into August already, with us a week behind schedule. Maybe you don't know that."

"You've told me this before," Bib Olsen said. "More than once. I admit we shore cain't bury them tracks under dirt with only our bare hands."

Zack spoke. "Our best chance is to easy them out of this place and trail them west until we can scout for a trestle or a bridge big enough so that we can try to push the herd underneath the tracks instead of over. If we mill around here much longer, a train might come along. That might scare the liver out of them, and they'd run."

"Train already comin'," Bib Olsen said.

Zack and his father whirled, staring in the direction Bib was pointing. A smudge of black smoke had appeared over the swells to the east. A train *was* coming.

Zack hit the saddle. "I'll stop it until we can move the herd out of range," he shouted. He headed the horse east along the railroad track, pushing the animal to a full gallop.

He had one factor in his favor. The approaching train was mounting one of the long swells in the plain, and the upgrade was telling on the wood-burning locomotive. It proved to be a combination train consisting of two passenger cars, a mail and baggage car and half a dozen box and flat cars. The thud of the exhaust from the coal-scuttle stack was growing more and more labored. Zack, as he rode into closer view, could see the heads of the engineer and the firemen poking from the windows, peering down at the slowing driving wheels.

The train was moving at a pace which Zack's horse could easily keep abreast of as he arrived alongside. The engineer was a young, redheaded man with a lantern jaw and hayrack shoulders, who sported a flaring red mustache.

"Stop it!" Zack yelled above the roar from the straining machinery. "We've got a trail herd sulled alongside the tracks ahead. You might stampede 'em, and we'd lose a lot of them most likely."

"What?"

Zack repeated his statement. The expression on the lantern-jawed engineer changed to disbelief, then to outraged scorn. "You don't think for a minute I'm goin' to stop a Rocky Mountain Express train just because some dumb Texas cowpoke has got some cattle grazing where they shouldn't be?" he screeched. "If I stopped this train on this grade, I'd have to back down five miles or more an' start over ag'in."

"We've got three thousand Longhorns on the prod," Zack yelled. "They're caught between the railroad tracks and the breaks. They might—"

The rawboned engineer was thumbing a nose at him. Zack snatched out his six-shooter. The engineer ducked out of sight, yelling profanity. Zack holstered the gun. He had been bluffing, having no intention of putting a bullet in the man.

The train, having topped the crest of the grade, was beginning to pick up momentum. Zack's horse began to lose ground. Passengers lined the opened windows of the two cars. Taunts and jeers were shouted at him as the cars moved ahead.

He tried to board the last car of the train, but his horse refused to move that close to the mechanical thing. The engineer was looking back from his window and making more insulting gestures.

"I'll look you up, my friend!" Zack panted. He knew the engineer could not hear the words but he was sure his intentions were plain, for the man clenched a fist and lifted it in a challenge.

The race had brought Zack back within sight of the herd. He could see his father and the crew riding frantically, trying to move the cattle as far from the track as possible, seeking to soothe them in preparation for the passing of the mechanical terror.

They might have succeeded in preventing a stampede, but the redhead at the throttle, leaning from the cab window so that he would not miss the spectacle, turned loose the whistle of the locomotive.

That did it. Zack uttered a moan. He kept moaning in pity as he watched. The blasting whistle had been the last straw. The cattle ran, scattering blindly away from the railroad track and the bellowing monster. Some headed back over the path by which they had entered the area. But one wing of the herd was stampeding blindly toward the coulees and alkali marshes.

Cold sweat in his clenched fists, Zack watched men ride clear of the cloud of dust that was kicked up by hundreds of hoofs. Will Nix, Bib Olsen, Johnny Summers, Juan Hernandez, Len Duvall. Others. All but one. All but one.

Then that one emerged from the dust and confusion and wearily dismounted. Zack drew a long breath, staring at his father, knowing the agony in Brandy Ben's heart. "Blast him," he mumbled weakly. "Why did he cut it so thin? He couldn't stop them. Nobody could."

He rode to his father's side. "You ought to have known better than to try to turn them," he raged. "Do you want to be buried in this forsaken country?"

Brandy Ben did not answer that. He sat watching helplessly as disaster piled upon disaster. "The poor critters!" he kept saying. "The poor, poor cattle!"

Zack discovered that tears were mingling with the dust on his father's unshaven cheeks. He sat humble. He had never before seen his father weep. He had never believed that tough, gruff Brandy Ben Keech was capable of tears.

He found himself forced to brush guiltily at his own eyes. Side by side, tall son, and weeping, graying father watched the cattle die. The coulees caught many of the stampeding Longhorns, piling them in heaps. Others were mired in the marshes, some moaning in terror as they sank until the sounds were smothered. Finally it was over.

"Two hundred head, give or take a half dozen or so," Zack told his father. "We came out of it better than I expected. We'll get an exact tally tomorrow, if they settle down."

It was sundown and they had succeeded in moving the

survivors of the stampede out of the trap and to safer distance from the right-of-way of the railroad.

"What did you say was the name of this railroad?" his father asked.

"Rocky Mountain Express, according to what the engineer said when I asked him to stop his train," Zack said.

"Never heard of it," Brandy Ben said.

"What's your plan?" Zack asked.

"If we can get these judheads movin' north again, I'll try to buy up enough beef at Ogallala or from ranches along the trail to fill out the herd. I still aim to make delivery date."

The cost of two hundred head to replace the lost cattle would come to at least six thousand dollars, and likely more, for prices would go up once the sellers realized that old Brandy Ben Keech had got his tail in a crack. It wasn't that he couldn't afford it. He owned a big outfit in Texas and had a reputation for reaping fat profits on trail herds he had been driving north for several years.

"First we've got to get these cattle across the track," Zack said. "I'll scout west of here and try to find a trestle or a bridge. Bib, you ride east in the morning."

They found a feasible path the next day where the Rocky Mountain Express bridged a wide riverbed which was mainly dry at this season. After waiting for two more days they chanced driving the cattle under the track, making sure there were no railroad trains due along that area at that time.

A talkative section hand who came by with three other workmen on a handcar furnished the trail men with that information and much more. As Brandy Ben had surmised, the Rocky Mountain Express, despite its fancy name, was considerably less than a major operation. It was independently owned and operated on some two hundred miles of track. Its traffic consisted of intermittent freight runs and a single combination train east and west daily.

"But if'n the Tollivers kin hang on long enough they'll be settin' purty," the man said. "The country's startin' to build up, with sodbusters an' cattlemen movin' in. An' if the Tollivers kin last it out, they'll tap them gold camps in the Rockies. Then their troubles will be over."

"Who are the Tollivers?" Zack asked.

"Cowboy, you sure must have lived fur out in the tules. You mean to say you never heerd of the Tollivers? Why, they've been railroad people since way back. J. K. Tolliver is president an' head of the board of the Rocky an' runs the railroad along with whatever other Tollivers air left. If it wasn't for them highbinders, they might make a million."

"Highbinders? What does that mean?"

The section hand suddenly became less talkative. He looked around as though to make sure his fellow workers had not been listening. He changed the subject abruptly.

"There's plenty of hustle in Sioux Wells," he said. "Town's growin' fast. Lots of action. They brung in Wild Bill Hickok a couple o' months ago to keep law an' order. I seen Wild Bill operate in Abilene a few years back. He's a tough man, but even he will need luck in Sioux Wells."

"Where is this Sioux Wells?" Zack asked.

"About thirty miles away. It's headquarters for the Rocky in these parts, but the main office is in Kansas City. As I was sayin', I saw Wild Bill tame some tough ones back in Abilene. He's somethin', he is."

Zack wasn't interested in Wild Bill Hickok, although he had heard of the man and his reputation. He did have interest in another person. "There's a Rocky Mountain Express engineer with red hair and a red mustache," he said. "About my size and age, I take it, with big teeth and a long nose. Do you happen to know that kind of a man?"

The section hand grinned. "That'd be Stan Durkin," he said. "I heerd about how he stampeded yore cattle. He was tellin' about it the other day in the Good Time, which is a first-class honky-tonk in the Wells. You wouldn't be wantin' to look him up an' try to take it out of his hide, now would you, Texas man?"

"Why would you think anything like that?" Zack asked.

"Forget it," the man said. "I'd hate to see a good-lookin' feller like you have his face mussed up permanent. Stan Durkin ain't never been licked in barroom or in the ring. He picks up some extra money fightin' all comers on Saturday nights at the Grizzly Bear Club, an' practices through the week on anybody who comes along, such as cowboys an' sheepherders. Take my advice an' steer clear of him."

"That's real considerate of you," Zack said. "I'll keep your words in mind."

After the cattle were safely north of the Rocky Mountain Express track Zack had Pinkie Lee, the Chinese cook, iron the wrinkles out of his going-to-town clothes and got out the polish to tone up his Sunday boots.

"Where you goin'?" his father demanded, discovering this activity.

"Make out your bill," Zack said.

"Bill?"

"A claim rather. A claim against the Rocky Mountain Express for six thousand dollars in loss of cattle. And a further statement that if this delay costs you penalty money on the delivery contract we'll bring a second claim against the railroad."

"Son," Brandy Ben said solicitously. "You're twenty-five years old, but you don't seem to know the facts of life. Railroads are owned by rich people what have high-priced lawyers to advise them. They pay the taxes that pay the salaries of judges an' lawmen. We got no more chance of gettin' a dollar out of a railroad up in this country than I have of yankin' up a piece o' sagebrush an' findin' a gold mine. Forget it. Next year we'll educate the cattle to railroads before headin' 'em north."

"I'll make out the claim myself," Zack said.

Brandy Ben sighed. "Do you think I don't know what's really gravelin' you? You're goin' in there to look up that railroad engineer what turned loose the whistle to spook the herd."

"Whatever gave you that notion?"

"I talked to that railroad hand too, son. I hear that this Stan Durkin is about the toughest knot in the timber. I don't reckon you'd stand for me goin' along with you?"

Zack gave his father a frosty look. "Or maybe Willie Nix," his father said hastily, naming the giant of the crew who had a reputation for brawling in cattle towns.

Zack did not answer. He saddled a horse and swung his war sack aboard. The section hand had said there was a sidetrack two or three miles west where the train to Sioux Wells could be flagged to pick up passengers.

Bib Olsen rode with him and kept relating stories about fools who had taken on more than they could handle, and had been crushed. "Just because you knocked out a few cowpokes in boxing matches at roundup camps don't mean you can stand up to every bucko that comes along," he said. "Remember that young professional pug what knocked you kicking in the second round at San'tone when you got too big fer your britches? If this railroader has got savvy enough to keep away from that right hand of yours, you're finished."

"Who said I aim to pick a fight?" Zack replied.

"I do," Bib sighed. "I only wish I could see it."

They found the siding, turned the faded red flag down, and settled down to wait. The train, two hours behind the schedule the section hand had mentioned, finally came creeping across the plain and ground to a stop. Stan Durkin was not at the throttle. The man handling that task was a plump, middle-aged individual.

Zack tossed his belongings aboard and followed them, leaving Bib to return his horse to the remuda. He stepped inside a coach and took a seat as the train jolted into motion again. A burly conductor came barging into the car, rattling a brass key chain that could be used as a bludgeon.

"Whar to, fella?" the man asked, instantly hostile as he saw that he was dealing with a cowboy, and a Texan at that.

"Sioux Wells," Zack said.

"One way?" the conductor asked, peering with a leer out at the empty plain.

"That'll do," Zack said, "though I doubt that I'll settle there."

"That'll be a dollar," the conductor said. "You a drover?"

"Nope," Zack said, paying the fare. "I'm a swatter."

"Swatter?"

"Fly swatter. A fly squats, I swat."

"Texans," the beefy man sniffed, and went away mumbling.

The majority of the seats in the car were occupied. Two painted ladies with false bangs hanging from beneath straw bonnets, sat midway in the car, one with high-buttoned shoe extended into the aisle. They were being ogled by two tough-nosed, swarthy passengers whom Zack tagged as cheap roughs whose specialty was likely to be back-alley muggings of unwary strangers. Both wore double-breasted shirts, striped breeches and boots of surprisingly good quality, and packed six-shooters in holsters, all of which seemed new and expensive.

Among the other passengers were the usual drummers

and business men and a homesteader with a wife and baby. An elderly woman and a young companion occupied a seat ahead of Zack. The elderly woman was small and gray-haired, with gold-rimmed spectacles and a tiny bonnet perched on the side of her head. She had knitting in her lap and her hands were busy.

Zack's attention turned to the small lady's companion and he sat up straighter. Even from the back, this one was a stunner. Thick, glossy hair, very dark. A nice, slender neck. Good, proud line of chin and cheek. She had animation, interest in the passing of even the drab sweep of buffalo grass. She turned once so that she glanced at Zack, and he felt that he was instantly appraised and found wanting. She had eyes to match her hair and manner. Snapfinger black eyes.

He hadn't seen a pretty girl in some time. Nor even a woman of any age or shape since the drive had laid over near Dodge for a few days, and that was far down the trail. He enjoyed just looking at the back of this one's lovely head.

Someone stirred from the heat apathy that claimed the passengers and exclaimed, "Antelope!"

A band of pronghorns had appeared out of the loneliness of the land and was bounding along with their stiff-legged, grasshopper gait, keeping pace with the train in what was an antelope's idea of a frolic.

One of the two roughs picked up a rifle that had been lying on the floor beneath his feet and moved to an unoccupied seat, lifting the window.

He raised the gun and fired twice. "Whoopee!" he screeched. "Got him! Busted his laig!"

The antelope were scattering and vanishing into the plain. All but one. This animal was hobbling on a bullet-broken front leg. The man emptied his rifle at the other fleeing animals. Zack could see the bullets kicking up puffs of dust around the target, but all shots evidently had missed.

The man, laughing shrilly, sank back in his seat. "I sure winged that ol' goat," he boasted. "Two hundred yards if it was an inch."

The train suddenly began to slow, the whistle sounding hoarsely ahead. Zack realized that the small, grandmotherly person had risen from her seat and had jerked the bell cord which was the signal to the engineer to bring the train to an emergency stop. The wheels ground to a halt.

"You just go out there and finish off that poor suffering beast," Grandma said to the tough with the rifle.

He looked at her, tobacco-stained teeth gaping, his hard face the picture of amazement. "What's that?" he mumbled.

"You heard me," Granny said. "Put some shells in that gun, pile off this car and finish what you never should have started in the first place."

The man glared disbelievingly, then began to laugh scornfully. "Go back to knitting your doilies, old lady," he said. "Do yuh think fer one minute thet I'd go out there in that hot sun and waste not only a ca'tridge but my time on a stnkin' goat? The world's full of pronghorns."

Granny lifted a folded parasol that had been leaning at her side and brought it down with a smart whacking sound on the tough's head. It came so unexpectedly that he had not even attempted to dodge. The blow drove his hat down around his ears. He reeled back in the seat, somewhat dazed.

The he recovered. He reared to his feet in a seething fury. "If you wasn't an old woman," he roared, "I'd . . ."

His voice thinned and faded off into nothing. He was looking into the maw of a derringer. It was in the hand of the beauty with the snapfinger dark eyes. It was a double-barreled weapon that Zack estimated was .50 caliber. At short range a slug of that size would tear a fearful hole in flesh. Two slugs would tear two holes.

The tough was aware of these possibilities. He cringed back. "What'n hell!" he croaked.

"Get off and finish that animal as my grandmother told you to do," the young lady said. She was the calmest person in the car, with the probable exception of her grandmother. Granny was inspecting her parasol. Satisfied that it had suffered no permanent damage, she laid it aside and said in a very positive voice, "Now git! An' don't waste any more time. This train's hours late already, and I'm growin' weary. Git out there an' do as any decent person ought to do."

The tough glared around. His stare was avoided by the eyes of other passengers who had ben jolted out of their heat torpor, and who obviously wanted no part of this. The man's glance finally rested on Zack—and remained there.

"Better do what the lady says," Zack said. "You're wasting our time."

Zack sat with his six-shooter muzzle resting on the back of the seat in front of him. The hammer was tilted back, but he was not pointing the pistol at anything in particular.

The tough turned to his companion, but found no sign of help there. "I cain't fight women!" he snarled. He gave Zack a glare and said, "I'll remember you, mister."

Reloading his rifle, he stumbled down the aisle and dropped off the train. From the window, Zack watched him head on foot through the hot grass to where the wounded antelope had halted at a distance, head drooping. Two shots sounded.

The peppery Granny peered from a window and said, "The poor, poor beast. At least its agony is over."

The heavy-jowled conductor came bursting into the

car. "Who pulled that bell cord?" he raged, his stomach vibrating.

"I did," Granny said calmly.

"You?" the conductor exploded unbelievingly. "Old lady, don't you know that—?"

"My name is Mrs. Julia Smith," Granny said. "And don't you know enough to take off your hat in the presence of ladies. Where was you brought up? In a pig sty?"

The conductor had to try several times before he could speak intelligibly. "Don't you know it's ag'in the law to stop a train carryin' the United States mail without permission of the conductor in charge—namely me?" he thundered.

"Fiddle-faddle," Julia Smith said. She picked up her knitting and seemed to lose interest in the conductor. Her granddaughter had returned the wicked derringer to whatever hiding place from which it had emerged. Zack suspected that it had come from a garter holster.

The tough returned, panting, hot and vengeful. He glared at Julia Smith and the handsome girl as he resumed his seat. He engaged in mumbled angry recrimination with his friend who was apparently denying all responsibility for his companion's humiliation. He gave Zack a scowl, but Zack only returned that with a beaming smile.

The conductor angrily yanked the bell rope twice. "You ain't heard the last of this, lady," he told Granny.

"Go polish your brass buttons," Granny said.

The train lurched ahead, couplings clashing.

Chapter 2

Zack holstered his six-shooter and relaxed in his seat. Julia Smith turned and thoroughly inspected him through the spectacles perched on her nose. Finally she lifted a hand, crooked an imperious finger, beckoning him to approach her. Irritated at her arrogant manner, he ignored her for a moment. Then he realized that this might be a chance to become acquainted with the granddaughter.

"What's your name?" Julia Smith asked.

"Keech," Zack said stiffly. "Anything else, ma'am?"

"A cowboy," she said. "I'd say south Texas by your accent. I don't like Texans and them from the south are the worst. They're pig-headed, rude."

"Texans don't cotton to other rude, mule-headed folks," Zack said. *"Adios!"*

"Keep your hair on," Julia Smith said. "In addition to your other shortcomings you're impudent also. And maybe stupid. I doubt if you knew what you might be letting yourself in for by horning in with me and my granddaughter against those two over there."

"I'll worry about that for at least five minutes," Zack said. He seized his chance and turned to the girl with the snapfinger dark eyes. "I didn't catch your name, miss."

Her smile was frigid. "How sad." She turned her back on him. Granny Smith gave him a leer, and he retreated to his seat, defeated.

The train built up to its top speed, which wasn't much. The roadbed seemed new and rough. The August after-

22

noon heat increased. The majority of the passengers sank back into their torpor and were tossed around in their seats. The buck-toothed, swarthy tough remained awake. He kept darting menacing glances at Zack and at Granny and her granddaughter, both of whom remained pointedly indifferent.

Granny turned in her seat and spoke to Zack so that everyone in the car could hear. "Stay out of dark alleys in Sioux Wells, Texas man," she said. "Stay sober. There are rats around, but if anythin' happens to you, I'll see to it that someone is strung up for it."

Zack grinned. "Thanks, ma'am. I'll remember."

That ended the glares and unvoiced threats. Silence came, except for the creaking and groaning of the train. Their route descended from the dry, higher plains and advanced into better, greener country, veined by creeks which fed a winding, small river. Homesteaders had taken over much of the land, and fields were lush with crops or pasture for cattle. The number of passengers in the two coaches indicated that the Rocky Mountain Express was doing a comfortable business.

The conductor returned on his rounds, carefully avoiding looking at Julia Smith. Zack accosted him.

"When was this railroad built?" he asked.

"Three, four years ago," the man said.

"Looks like it's doing pretty good."

"It might look that way, but it ain't," the man growled.

"How's that? This country seems to be filling in."

"The country's doin' fine. What's needed is half a dozen good hangin's."

"Hangings? Why?"

Like the section hand a few days earlier, the conductor grew cautious. He looked around, then ended the conversation and hurried away.

Zack settled back, frowning. Evidently the Rocky Mountain Express's outward appearance of prosperity was tarnished. If so, he began to suspect that this would go against his chances of collecting his claim.

However, there was this J. K. Tolliver whom the section hand had named as head of the railroad. Zack had been brought up to believe that all railroad presidents were rich beyond imagination. He had never met a railroad president, nor any rich easterner, as a matter of fact. What few tenderfeet he had encountered were weirdly garbed tourists who were as likely as not to mount a horse from the Indian side, and get kicked over the corral bars. It was very probable that J. K. Tolliver was wealthy enough to pay an honest claim against his railroad, no matter what the situation of the railroad itself. It occurred to Zack that he might have to travel east and take it up with J. K. Tolliver in person. That gave him cold chills. Not because of J. K. Tolliver. He had heard of people coming to no good end in those crowded eastern cities.

"Sioux Wells!" the conductor bellowed, returning to the car. "Sioux Wells, next stop!"

Passengers, including Zack, aroused and began groping for their luggage. Grandma Julia Smith stored her knitting in a handbag. Her gorgeous granddaughter, who had fallen asleep, was arranging her hair and pinning on a small straw bonnet trimmed with daisies.

When the train ground to a stop, Zack shouldered his belongings and alighted on a plank platform which flanked a two-story depot whose upper floors evidently contained the offices of the railroad. He looked at Sioux Wells beyond the station. Sioux Wells looked back at him. The settlement was a one-street, one-sided stringtown that stretched along the railroad yards for a considerable distance. The tracks narrowed to a pin point in the distance, and were swallowed by the glare of the sun. At Zack's back were sidetracks, cattle corrals and chutes and idle rolling stock. He could make out the faint dots that were the soddies and shacks of settlers here and there in the distance.

East of the depot were freight sheds. Great ricks of buffalo bones were stacked along the tracks awaiting shipment to eastern grinding plants. A stack of buffalo hides, dry as wood, made its odorous presence known. The great herds were about done for in this region and their bones now served as a source of income for the settlers.

A buffalo hunter, a rare specimen now, was just in, and his two swampers were unloading fresh hides at the buyer's yard across from the railroad station. The hunter had a jug of whiskey in his hand, which he passed up to the swampers. From appearances the jug had been going the rounds very liberally, for the hunter pulled his Sharp's buffalo rifle from the wagon, loaded it and peered around for a target.

He found one and fired. Zack heard feminine screams of outrage from somewhere down the street. A stream of water was spurting from a wooden water tank that was mounted on the roof of a two-story building whose sign proclaimed it as the Good Time Music Hall. Heads appeared from the upper windows, using language that ladies do not utter.

The hunter lowered his rifle and hid it back of him, grinning into his month's growth of ragged beard, acting for all the world the picture of innocence. But the haze of powder smoke that hovered overhead betrayed him. A pistol appeared in front of one of the feminine heads at a window. The hunter ducked in time and the slug from the pistol only whacked into the load of buffalo hides. The pistol kept roaring, but the hunter and the swampers had disappeared back of the wagon.

"Hey, Gussie!" the hunter yelled. "Quit smokin' us up, afore you hurt somebody. Cain't you take a joke?"

A tall, long-haired man wearing an immaculate white shirt, string tie and an expensive Panama hat, appeared from a gambling house. A marshal's badge was pinned to a suspender. "Quit it, Gussie!" he shouted. "It's Ed Hake again. I'll see to it he pays for any damages. He's been on the buffalo range for weeks an' is just havin' a little fun."

The speaker was equipped with a brace of pistols in holsters that had ben made with an eye to permitting a quick draw.

"By glory, it *is* Wild Bill!" one of the train arrivals nearby said. "I heard he was marshal here, but didn't believe it."

Order was restored instantly in Sioux Wells. The heads withdrew from the windows after another barrage of language at soprano pitch.

"Be in court in the mornin' to pay fine and damages, Ed," the marshal said to the buffalo hunter, and then headed back to his interrupted game in the gambling house.

A man appeared on the roof of the music hall, set up a ladder, and plugged the bullet hole in the water tank, ending the spurt of liquid. Evidently this was not the first time the tank had been a target. Zack could make out other plugs in its sides. He heard a windmill pump begin operating to refill the tank. Apparently the Good Time had very up-to-date facilities. Zack had heard that some establishments up north had running water in the rooms. It came out of faucets through pipes. He had to see this with his own eyes.

Grandma Julia Smith and her granddaughter assembled their baggage, not lacking assistance from male bystanders, and boarded a waiting hack that carried them away toward a hotel, which like the Good Time, was a frame, weatherboarded structure with a water tank on its roof too.

Zack walked across the street toward the Good Time. He was thirsty and was thinking of a cold, foaming mug of beer. He stepped through the swing doors and headed for the bar, which was unexpectedly elegant with a glossy, varnished surface and polished brass rails. The big, mirrowed backbar sported pyramids of glassware.

There were several patrons at the bar, glasses before them, smoke curling from their cigars and pipes. They wore denim jackets, striped caps and pants to match, and heavy brogans. Railroad men.

One was the big lantern-jawed, redheaded engineer who had been at the throttle when the K-Bar-K herd had been stampeded. Stan Durkin. He had a mug of beer in his hand and was holding the floor, relating some tale which his listeners were not interrupting. Zack gained the impression that Stan Durkin was in the habit of dominating the conversation.

Zack placed his belongings on a chair at a poker table that was covered and not in use at this hour. He unbuckled his gun belt and hung it over the back of the chair. It was evident that Stan Durkin was unarmed. In any event Zack felt that this matter required something more satisfying than gunplay.

Stan Durkin was unaware of Zack's arrival. He was reaching the climax of his narrative, and his listeners were waiting with fixed attention. Durkin was a big man, taller than Zack by maybe an inch and many pounds heavier. His long arms were knobbed by big hands. His nose had been broken more than once and there were a few white scars along the jawline and a permanent one in crimson above his right cheekbone. He had seen considerable fistic action, as the section hand had mentioned.

Zack tapped him briskly on the shoulder, halting the tale at its important point. Durkin, with an impatient snort, tried to continue without turning to look at his annoyer. Zack tapped him again on the shoulder—harder. Much harder. So hard it jolted Durkin into realization that trouble was hunting him.

He whirled, rage boiling in his eyes. "What the hell do *you* want?" he roared.

"Remember me?" Zack asked.

Durkin peered. Rcollection began to dawn.

"Yeah," Zack said. "You didn't kill any humans the other day. Otherwise I'd be even meaner than I aim to be. But you cost us around two hundred head of cattle. I'm here to collect for the loss from the railroad and to take the interest out of your ugly hide."

Stan Durkin believed that offense was the best defense. "Why, you fool!" he snarled. "I'll beat you to a pulp, cowpoke."

He began moving in on Zack, swaying on the balls of his feet. But a man moved between them, shoving them away from each other. The intruder was Wild Bill Hickok.

"No fightin' in here, gentlemen," the marshal said, and Zack was surprised by the softness of his voice. "All you'd do is wreck glassware an' tables. Take it outside if you've got to settle whatever is in your craws. There's plenty of room in the street. And there'll be no foul fightin'. No gougin', kneein' or jumpin' on a man when he's down. I'll decide when one or the other has had enough."

"I couldn't be happier," Stan Durkin said. "I'll wipe up Railroad Street with him."

Durkin led the way outside, followed by Zack, Wild Bill and every person in the place, including the bartenders. The marshal picked a likely spot in the dusty street and said, "All right. Go to it."

Nearby stood the hotel. It sported a veranda at the front equipped with chairs and a porch swing. Granny Smith's granddaughter came from the lobby and stood on the porch. With her was a good-looking man in a neat business suit and starched collar.

"Better go inside, ma'am," Wild Bill said, lifting his

Panama. "There's goin' to be some roughin' around here. Not a sight for ladies."

The girl with the snapfinger eyes spoke. "I've got ten dollars that says the railroad man wins."

There was silence. Zack spoke. "I'll take the bet, ma'am. Cash."

"It'll be easy money, miss," Stan Durkin said, bowing grandly in the direction of the girl. "This won't take long."

He and Zack faced each other in the dusty street, circling for a space, measuring each other. Durkin came in, feinting, dancing, displaying fistic experience. Zack stood, his fists only half-raised, as though he was timid. That encouraged Durkin into the belief that he had an unskilled victim.

Durkin charged. He was confident. He presented a shoulder, crossed with a left, and expected his opponent to be in position for a knockout with the right. Zack had fallen for some such maneuver himself one evening in the past in a makeshift ring in San Antonio when he had the temerity to get into the ring with a young professional pugilist who was picking up spending money by barnstorming through the hinterlands.

Durkin swung the right just as Zack had swung at the professional pug that night. Durkin missed, just as Zack had missed. However, a fist did connect. But it was Zack's right and not Durkin's. It landed on Durkin's jaw, and it had back of it all of Zack's strength.

Durkin stood a moment, swaying, a glassy look in his eyes. Zack refrained from swinging again, for he had seen that same vacancy in the expressions of other men on whose jaws he had connected solidly.

Then Durkin pitched on his face. He did not move.

Dead, unbelieving silence descended on Railroad Street. The faces of the girls who crowded the upper windows of the Good Time remained fixed there. Julia Smith's granddaughter and her companion stared from the veranda of the hotel. No one spoke. All eyes were on the recumbent body of Stan Durkin.

Wild Bill broke the silence. "I reckon there's no point in countin' him out." He bent over Durkin. "He might have a busted or dislocated jaw," he said. "Some of you boys better pack him to a doctor. Fetch a stretcher. There's one at the depot."

One of the railroad men spoke resentfully to Zack. "You must have got in a lucky lick, mister. Ain't nobody could knock out Stan Durkin like that with one punch unless there was somethin' crooked about it. You likely had somethin' wrapped up in yore fist. Let's take a look."

"Sure," Zack said. He moved close and let the man see that his right hand was empty. Then he clenched the fist and knocked the man as cold as Stan Durkin with one blow.

Howls of fury arose. The bystanders surged in. "We'll fix him! He cain't come into this town an—"

They surged back. They found themselves facing, not Zack, but Hickok. He hadn't drawn his guns—as yet.

"I'll take care of this," he said. "He's guilty of assault an' battery, but this feller here asked fer it. He questioned this man's integrity an' got what was comin' to him if you ask me. But he'll have to pay a fine. Five an' costs will likely cover it when he faces the justice. Meanwhile, I'm releasin' him on his own recognizance, an' I don't want no mob talk from nobody. You hear me?"

They heard him. He addressed Zack. "Keep out of any more trouble while you stay in Sioux Wells, which stay I hope will be short. What's your name?"

"Name's Keech," Zack said. "I've got business here, an' I don't aim to leave until it's settled."

Hickok looked him over from head to foot. He had sad eyes, expressionless eyes on the gray-green side. Zack had heard that this man had killed at least a dozen persons.

"You're a sassy rooster," Hickok said in his mild voice. "Be at the justice court at nine o'clock tomorrow mornin' to pay your fine."

A stretcher was brought and Stan Durkin was carried away. He was already reviving, and Zack was sure he had suffered no more damage than a jaw that would be swollen for a few days.

Zack got his war sack and gun belt from the Good Time and headed for the hotel, whose name was Traveler's Rest, according to the sign on the veranda.

To his dismay he found half a dozen wide-eyed, barefoot urchins tagging along at his heels. They were nudging each other and whispering that this was the man who had licked Stan Durkin.

Zack was embarrassed. "Go home, lads," he pleaded. "Don't they teach manners to young ones in this town?"

The youngsters dropped a dozen paces back, but that was all. They gathered around the steps of Traveler's Rest as Zack mounted to the veranda. The dark-haired girl and her male companion were still on the veranda. So was Wild Bill Hickok.

Hickok turned and discovered he was blocking Zack's path. He said, "Here's the winner, ma'am. He cost you ten dollars, I reckon, but I suppose you want to congratulate him."

"I certainly do," the girl said. "First the ten dollars. He seems to have earned it."

Her companion tried to move in, reaching for his wallet. She pushed him back. "It's my pleasure," she said, and produced a gold piece from her reticule and handed it to Zack.

Then she brought the heel of her slipper down very forcefully on the toe of Zack's boot. The slipper was high-heeled.

"And congratulations," she said. "Come, Frank."

She swept past, drawing her companion with her, and vanished into the lobby. He was a well-proportioned man in his thirties, Zack judged. He gave Zack an amused smile as he passed by. Zack watched them mount to the second floor.

Not until then would he permit himself to give any sign of pain. "O—oo-f-f!" he groaned. He dropped the war sack and grabbed at his foot, dancing around until the pain subsided.

"Why'd she do that?" he asked Hickok. "She's a right hard loser."

"There's only one thing you can take for granted about a female," Hickok said. "They'll always be cantankerous an' flighty when you figure you got 'em estimated as all sugar an' spice. Especially the lookers."

Hickok strolled away in the direction of the gambling house from which he had originally emerged.

Chapter 3

Zack entered the lobby, still favoring his foot. The wrinkled, turkey-necked man back of the counter eyed him without warmth and said, "I suppose you want a room. That'll be five dollars a night."

"Your sign says rooms are a dollar to a dollar and a half a night," Zack said. "I'll take the best. I need a shave an' a bath. That's another two-bits, according to the sign."

The hotel man wanted to refuse. Several railroad men had mounted to the veranda and were peering into the lobby with scowls. But he looked at Zack's face and did not have the sand.

"I'm anxious to see this water running out of a pipe that I've heard about," Zack said as he picked up the change from the gold piece he had won from the girl. He looked at the key and the tag attached which indicated that his room was Number 209.

He mounted the stairs and found the room which was midway down the hall. A sign at the rear and an arrow pointed to the bathing facilities.

The room was average, with a limp rag rug on oiled pine flooring, a bed, commode and a rack for hanging clothes. Zack lost no time getting out his shaving material and heading down the hall.

A wizened flunky came stumping from downstairs and handed him soap and a towel. "Don't waste water, mister," he warned. "I'm here to see that if you do you'll pay another quarter."

Zack shaved, amazed at the convenience of a wall basin into which sun-heated water was piped. The bathing equipment was equally novel. A pipe jutted from the ceiling. When he turned on a faucet, water sprayed from a perforated gadget. He had never before taken a bath standing up. He stood beneath the spray so long that the flunky came to the door and informed him he would have to come up with another two-bit piece.

Zack finally emerged, toweled himself and got into fresh clothes that he had brought from his war bag. "What do you do in winter to make folks comfortable under that thing?" he asked the attendant.

"Winter? We close up this here thing. Anybody in need of a bath in winter kin wallow in a tub. Feller, it gits down to forty below in these parts at times."

Zack, refreshed, headed down the hall toward his room. Deep twilight was at hand, but the one lamp in the hall had not yet been lighted. A man emerged from a room toward the front of the hall and came brushing past him. He was Wild Bill Hickok. Zack, surprised, said, "Howdy, Marshal!"

Wild Bill replied briefly and moved past. He left by way of a rear door which led to an outer stairway at the back of the building. Zack had the impression that the marshal had not particularly wanted to be recognized. Evidently he had come to the Traveler's Rest instead of the gambling house, and must have entered by the rear stairway while Zack had been in the shower.

Zack heard faint voices and laughter from the room from which Hickok had emerged. Feminine voices. A man's voice. The girl with the wonderful dark eyes, of course, and the man who had met her at the hotel. He made out the more positive voice of the grandmother. Hickok apparently had been a visitor in the quarters of Julia Smith and her kin.

Zack's toes on his right foot still smarted. There was

a small bruise to charge up to the granddaughter. He
shrugged, and unlocked the door of his room. He had left
his wallet, his watch and other pocket possessions in the
bureau drawer and had hung his gun belt on a wall peg.
The key to his door was a cheap skeleton affair, a dupli-
cate of which could be bought in any hardware store.

A shadow warned him in time and he was fading away,
ducking as the first of his assailants came at him. The
man was swinging a club. It grazed Zack's shoulder, doing little damage. Driving a fist from a crouch he felt it
bury in the man's stomach. He felt great satisfaction as
he heard the gushing moan of agony. He rolled aside,
certain that this one, at least, would be out of it for a few
minutes.

The second man was braced to move in. He also had
a club—a wagon spoke—in his hands. He was the buck-
toothed one who had come out second best with Granny
Smith in the matter of the wounded antelope. The one
who was slumped on the floor, gasping agonizingly for
breath, had been Bucktooth's seat-mate on the train.

Bucktooth lost his ambition. The door was open. He
wheeled and tore through it, abandoning his partner. Zack
lunged, trying to tackle him but missed and sprawled on
the floor. He came to his feet, but was tangled in the rag
rug. He skidded and fell again. By the time he got into
the hall his quarry had vanished through the rear door.
Zack could hear him taking the downsteps in long leaps.

Zack raced in pursuit. Dusk was deepening into darkness. He did not risk a broken leg leaping down the
stairs as his quarry had done. He could hear receding
footsteps. The man was vanishing among a maze of barns
and corrals, heading toward the railroad yards evidently.
Zack ran in that direction for a time, then realized it was
useless.

He came hurrying back to the hotel, mounted the
steps and ran down the hall. The door of his room was

still open. Granny Smith, her granddaughter and the dark-haired man, along with several other hotel guests, were peering into his room. They parted to let Zack through. The open window told the story. Bucktooth's partner had recovered enough to drop from the window, which was a comparatively short descent, and had fled.

"What'n blazes happened?" Granny Smith asked waspishly. "It sounded like a buffalo stampede."

"I had visitors," Zack said. "They were friends of yours, by the way. They seemed to have a grudge to settle with me, and all the time you were the one who made them eat crow."

"You're talking about the bully boys who was on the train," Granny said. "I warned you to look out for 'em, now didn't I?"

Hickok had heard the commotion at the hotel and had returned. "What did they look like?" he asked.

Granny Smith supplied the descriptions quickly and accurately. Trashy, mean-looking as wet skunks. One's got teeth like a gopher, an' his pal's pitted with pockmarks. Both need a bath and a shave—an' a rope around their necks. Both about thirty, cotton shirts, denim pants, cowboots. Armed, dangerous."

"You've got a mind for detail," Hickok said. "If they're still in town, which I doubt, I'll run 'em in."

He eyed Zack. "You're right busy, my friend. You hit town only a couple of hours ago, and you've been in two ruckuses already. What did you say your name is?"

"Keech," Zack said. "Zachary Taylor Keech."

"You wouldn't be related to an old Texas hellion named Ben Keech, who's better known as Brandy Ben, now would you?"

"He's my dad," Zack said. "You acquainted with him?"

Hickok smiled. "I've bumped into Brandy Ben a time or two. First time at Abilene, if I recollect. Later on, he come through Baxter Springs with a drive when I was stayin' over there a few days. Would you take it kindly if I asked you just why you're in Sioux Wells?"

"Same reason why I had the ruckus with that Durkin fellow," Zack said. "I came here to press a claim for six thousand dollars against the Rocky Mountain Express Railway. Durkin stampeded our herd some days ago, and we lost around two hundred head."

He became aware that a strained silence had come. Everyone was looking, rather embarrassed, at the natty, dark-mustached, dark-haired man who stood with one hand laid possessively on the arm of the handsome girl.

He looked at Zack and laughed. "It happens that I'm Frank Niles, superintendent of the Rocky," he said. "I'm the man who will have to handle your claim." He laughed again, tolerantly. "Six thousand dollars, you say. For cattle that our engineer was supposed to have stampeded. Well, that *is* quite a claim. This is hardly the place for us to discuss it. Come to the office tomorrow, Mr. Keech, and we'll see what can be done."

Zack understood that Frank Niles was already of a mind not to pay that amount of money, and, in fact, no money at all. The group broke up. Granny and Frank Niles and the girl returned to the suite at the front. Zack entered his room and took stock. His wallet, watch and pistol were still in place. His assailants had not had the time to rob him.

He left the room, locking the door, and descended to the street, heading for an eating place which was some distance away. He found Hickok waiting for him.

The marshal fell in step with him, and they strolled along. "About that claim against the railroad," Hickok said. "You must know that you've got as much chance as an icicle on a hot stove."

"Would it help if I got a lawyer?" Zack asked.

"Ain't a lawyer in five hundred miles that would

touch you," Hickok said. "And in Sioux Wells, least of all. This is a railroad town. The bread and butter of most everybody here comes from sidin' in with the railroad—or stealin' from it."

"Stealing?"

"That's another story," Hickok said.

"It's a fair claim," Zack said. "If Durkin hadn't touched off the whistle, the boys likely would have been able to have held the run down to where it wouldn't have amounted to much."

"You're buttin' a stone wall," Hickok said. "All I can do is wish you luck. For one thing, the Rocky couldn't come up with six thousand dollars right now, even if you got a judgment handed down from the Almighty."

"How's that? Why, six thousand dollars ought to be pocket change for a railroad."

"Not with the Rocky," the marshal said. "If things keep goin' as they have been, the Rocky will be bankrupt or in receiver's hands before long."

"Everybody says railroads make piles of money," Zack said.

"That'll be news to most of 'em, and to the Rocky above all. The Rocky had enough trouble with Indians in summer an' blizzards in winter buildin' into this country without bein' plagued by these highbinders just when they might have seen their way clear."

"I've heard this mentioned before," Zack said. "Just what is a highbinder?"

"Thieves is a better word for them," Hickok said. "They started out a couple of years ago as petty robbers, stealin' a packin' crate from a boxcar here an' there. Then they got bolder an' began stealin' by the carload."

"Carload? How did they get away with that?"

"They got bolder an' bolder. They ditched a freight train east of here less than a year ago, an' got away with enough freight to load a dozen wagons. The engine crew was killed in the wreck, an' they murdered the conductor and a brakeman. They didn't want any witnesses who knew them. They seem to know when there's valuable freight aboard, an' that's when they strike."

"What kind of valuable freight?"

"They got a carload of sewing machines, cookstoves an' kitchenware in one haul. Worth plenty in the mining camps that are boomin' in the Rockies. Miners are hittin' it rich, an' their wives want the best that money can buy. Another time they got away with a carload of lighter stuff—women's dresses, shoes, things they wear underneath, hats, bustles an'—"

"Bustles?"

"Don't tell me you don't know what a bustle is?"

"Of course I do," Zack snorted. "Do you think we live in caves down in Texas? They're contraptions that ladies wear to make 'em look—well, make 'em look more important. But what kind of robbers would bother with stealing things like that?"

"That shows your ignorance," Hickok said. "These particular objects came from New York, an' was wholesaled at three dollars apiece. There was a thousand of them, along with crates of slippers, dresses an' all the other truck that females need to keep 'em happy. About seven thousand dollars' worth, in all. Then they got into another car which had ten crates of Remington magazine rifles, late models. Twelve rifles to a crate at fifty dollars a gun, wholesale. They got a dozen kegs of Galena lead an' five kegs of DuPont powder. All that run into money. Close to ten thousand dollars, all of which the Rocky was liable for."

"What in blazes do they do with all that stuff?"

"Some of it is being sold right here in Sioux Wells," Hickok said. "Some in Denver, some in Hays City. Likely the bulk of it goes back to Kansas City where there's a bigger market. It's shipped back over the Santa Fe and the Union Pacific, or maybe even the Rocky, labeled as pickled buffalo tongue or some such. It just vanishes onto store shelves where it's sold cheap an' fast, but at a big profit, for it don't cost much. It's a leetle difficult, for instance, to identify a stolen bustle when a lady is wearin' it."

"How often do things like that happen?"

"Too danged often. An' it's growin' worse. They are gettin' bolder. They got away with forty thousand dollars in gold dust just about six weeks ago."

"Forty thousand?"

"It had been brought by wagon out of the minin' camps to a little station forty miles west of here that is the end of steel for the Rocky. It was to be shipped to the mint in Philadelphia. The highbinders ditched the train, killed another railroad man, an' got away with the dust. Nobody but a few was supposed to know it was aboard."

"You're trying to make it sound like I'm picking on a poor, ragged-bottom railroad that's on its way to the poorhouse," Zack snorted.

"Well, it's something like that," Hickok admitted.

"How about this J. K. Tolliver, who's said to be the big augur back of this outfit?" Zack sniffed. "Likely he's rolling in gold notes or such somewhere back east, living off the honey and fruit of the land. He's the one I aim to gun for. I reckon he's in the clear like most of these sharpers who let other folks take the losses."

Hickok gave him a slanting look. "The Tollivers own about all there is of the stock in the Rocky," he said. "It's a family affair. This here railroad ain't in the same class with the U.P. or the Santa Fe. It was dreamed up by a Tolliver an' built by the Tollivers who've put all their money into it."

Zack eyed the marshal. "Why are you telling me this sad story about the Tollivers, Mr. Hickok?" he demanded. "I don't like to pick on a man when he's in trouble, but this railroad still owes my father six thousand dollars. I aim to collect."

"Of course, of course," Hickok said. "I ain't usually in the habit of sounding off to a stranger. Maybe I sort of cottoned to you from the way you took care of Stan Durkin. I liked the way you leveled him with one punch, with all his friends around. It reminded me of a friend of mine who is a law man in Dodge City the last I heard of him. Name of Earp. Wyatt Earp. I saw him hit a man who had it comin' an' lay him low with one punch, just as you did. Have you ever considered goin' into the ring? Prize fightin' for money?"

"I tried it once," Zack said. "I was knocked kicking. I'm a cowman from here on in. That's my trade."

"How are you with a gun?"

"Gun?"

"Ever shoot a man? Ever have to draw in earnest?"

"That's sort of a leading question, isn't it, marshal?"

"It's not idle curiosity," Hickok said. "You've got the earmarks of a man who'd make a good law officer. You've shown that you can use your fists. You might have to use something faster than fists if you decided to take over this badge I'm wearin'."

Zack was out of his depth. "Wait a minute! Who said anything about—?"

"I'm here only temporarily," Hickok said. "I took over this law job as a favor to J. K. Tolliver, who is an old friend."

"You know J. K. Tolliver? In person?"

"Yes. J. K. Tolliver hoped I'd be able to break up this gang of highbinders. It was a tougher job than I had expected."

Zack eyed the marshal. "If you couldn't swing it, you could hardly expect a greenhorn like me to do it, now could you?"

"The trouble is," Hickok explained, "they knew just why I came here an' took the job. They know every move I make. If I could drop out of sight, I might be able to ramble around and maybe get some information on these thieves. But somebody's got to wear the badge."

He paused for a space, then added, "The fact is that I'll be dead if I hang around here much longer. I've been lucky this far."

"You mean they've tried to—"

A gun blasted a spurt of flame from between buildings down the street. Hickok's hat was knocked slanting over his ear. The gun exploded again, but by that time both Hickok and Zack were diving flat on the sidewalk.

Hickok was firing as he fell, a chilling demonstration of his reputation for gun speed. Both of his six-shooters were thundering, raking the blackness from which the attack had come. Zack's gun was in his own hand, but he held his fire, awaiting the outcome of Hickok's volley.

The guns went silent. The echoes quit bouncing from the town's walls and nearby windows ceased shuddering in their frames. Zack could now hear the sickening, agonized breathing of a dying man.

Hickok ran, crouching, down the sidewalk and halted at the corner of a building, listening to sounds from the darkness. "You there," he called. "Come out!"

The burbling sound continued. Hickok reloaded his guns, then advanced cautiously into the darkness. He returned dragging a limp body with him. In the lamplight from the windows of a nearby gambling house Zack looked down at a hard-faced man, a stranger. The tough was breathing his last. Life faded from him in a convulsive quiver of fingers and legs.

"Name of Glover," Hickok said. "He's been a barfly around here. One of the highbinders, of course. Paid to get me. If I'd stopped that slug he might have tried to knock you over."

"Why me?"

"He runs in the same herd with the two who laid for you in your room."

"You mean those two are highbinders too?"

"The one with the big teeth calls himself the Ogallala Kid. His pal goes by the name of Matt Pecos. Likely he's never been within five hundred miles of the Pecos River. Their specialty is wrecking trains and robbing boxcars."

"You know that for sure?"

"I know it, and I know half a dozen more like them and Glover who hang out here in Sioux Wells are in on it too. But knowing it in your mind and catchin' them red-handed so it can be proved in court are a long piece apart. What the Tollivers are after are the brains back of these fellers. These are small fry, who only take orders. Someone who plans the jobs has a lot of gray matter between his ears. That's the one—or ones—the Tollivers want."

A crowd gathered. The majority were railroad men. They stood gazing down at the twisted body of the dead man. Someone in the rear spoke, "Another notch on Hickok's gun."

The majority of the gathering shifted uneasily. No other voice was raised to back up the unseen speaker.

Hickok ignored the matter. "Send for Doc Appleton," he said. "Tell him it's a coroner's job this time."

The medical man arrived and asked the routine questions, for he also served as coroner. When he was finished, Hickok motioned Zack, and they moved away from the crowd.

"I withdraw my request," Hickok said.

"For what?"

"For askin' a man to make a target of himself in my place. I'll stick to the job here 'til it's finished, one way or another. What I was really wantin' was a chance to look around to see if I could find out what's happened to a friend of mine."

"Friend?"

"Name of Mel Sanders. Around here he was known as Jimmy Broom. I talked him into comin' to Sioux Wells not too long ago to see if he could get some information on these highbinders. He used to be a deputy under me back in Abilene. An' a good one. He acted the part of a bum, sweepin' out saloons, an' hangin' around honky-tonks. He dropped out of sight four days ago."

"The highbinders? They got onto him?"

Hickok shrugged wearily. "If so, God help him. And God help them if they've done away with him."

He changed the subject abruptly. "See to it that you show up in court tomorrow," he said. "At nine, o'clock, sober. You've got to answer charges of disturbin' the peace."

Chapter 4

"Five dollars an' costs, which makes a total of seven dollars," the justice of the peace said, slapping a palm down on the table which served as his bench.

The courtroom was part of the marshal's office and the jail. Zack fished in his pocket, found a ten dollar gold piece, which brought a frown from the court.

"Five an' costs an' three dollars for contempt of court," the justice thundered. He was a bald-headed buzzard of a man.

"Contempt of court?" Zack questioned incredulously.

"For not appearin' in this court with the proper change," the justice said.

Zack was crimson with rage. But he happened to look at Wild Bill Hickok who was hiding a grin back of a hand. The marshal wagged his head, warning him to be silent and accept the verdict.

Zack retreated to the spectator's benches, scowling. The judge called the next defendant who happened to be the buffalo hunter, Ed Hake, who had punctured the hole in the water tank on the roof of the Good Time. Hake pleaded guilty.

"Ten dollars an' costs," the justice thundered. "I ought to give you thirty days, Ed, but it happens our jail is full right now, lucky for you. An' another ten dollars to Gussie Bluebell for damages to her dress from water which came down through the ceiling, an event for which you were responsible."

"Here's your ten bucks an' two fer costs," Hake said

45

amiably. "I'll deliver the ten dollars to Gussie in person an' glad to do it. Me an' Gussie air old friends."

"Oh, no you don't!" his honor snarled. "I'll see to it myself that Gussie gets paid. Put that other ten dollars here on the judicial bench alongside the fine an' costs."

Zack and Hickok retreated from the courtroom into the marshal's small office. "Some day a real lawyer is goin' to wrap that old devil up in graft charges until he'll never be able to talk his way out," Hickok chuckled. "But it's only penny-ante stuff."

He lowered his voice. "We're out for bigger game. Are you still of a mind to insist that the Rocky owes your dad six thousand dollars?"

"I sure am," Zack said. "I'm more than insisting. I want that money."

"I happen to know that J. K. Tolliver has offered five thousand dollars to anyone who figures out a way to put an end to these highbinders," Hickok said. "I reckon the ante could be tilted to six thousand."

Zack crocked a cynical eye at the marshal. "Now I've heard everything. The railroad owes me six thousand dollars. It's a legitimate claim. But you've got the gall to ask me to risk a bullet in the back by gumshoeing around, acting like a detective or something. Just to earn what's honestly coming to me."

"That's right," Hickok said mildly. "But it happens that I'm not the one who's asking you to take on the job."

"Who, then?"

"J. K. Tolliver."

Zack stared disbelievingly. "Now, wait a minute. How could a big gun like that know anything about me?"

"That's beside the point," Hickok said. "But it's true. Frank Niles can vouch for it."

"Niles? The white-collar man I saw with the pretty girl at the hotel?"

"As superintendent of the railroad he's in close touch

with J. K. Tolliver, naturally," Hickok said. "Niles knows all about this."

Zack pretended to clap a hand to his forehead in bewilderment. "Let's go over this again. I came to Sioux Wells only yesterday as a Texas trail driver to press a claim for damages against this railroad. I gathered from the way Niles acted yesterday that he had decided I was wasting my time. Now I'm being asked to risk being killed just to pull the railroad's chestnuts out of the fire."

"Six thousand dollars," Hickok said. "It's the only way you'll ever get the money. You can't squeeze water out of a stone, nor money out of a railroad near bankruptcy."

He added, "My advice is for you to forget the six thousand and clear out of Sioux Wells."

"You'd make a good trout fisherman," Zack growled. "You know how to whip a fly just above the water. You know I won't clear out."

"I generally catch a few when I go fishing," Hickok admitted.

"This time it's a sucker you're after, not a trout," Zack said.

"Get moving," Hickok said.

"Where to?"

"Down to the railway station to have a talk with Frank Niles. His office is upstairs above the waitin' room."

"What would we talk about?"

"Your claim, for one thing."

"Something tells me that won't be all, nor even the most important part of it. I take it he's expecting me."

"Yes. It would be best for you to walk right down the street and ask the man in the ticket office how to get to Niles' office. Ask it so that anybody around can hear it."

"Sort of advertise that I'm calling on Niles to demand my money. Is that it?"

"It's pretty well known already why you came to Sioux

Wells," Hickok said. "You've established yourself as not among the Rocky Mountain Express's fondest admirers. First you level their star fistfighter with one punch. You have made it known that you're here to collect that money, even if you have to take it out of somebody's hide. It would only look like common sense for you to take on Niles this morning at his office to lay down the law to him."

Zack eyed the marshal in silence for a time. "I've got the feeling I'm being led around like a bull with a ring in his nose," he said. "As a matter of fact, I had in mind a visit with this Niles gentleman as first order of business. Now, I find it's all been arranged."

"Then I'm wasting my time talking to you," Hickok said jovially, slapping him on the back. "Here's luck. By the way, don't take Frank too lightly. He wears a stiff collar and dresses like a dude, but he might not be as easy to level as Stan Durkin. I happen to know he can take care of himself in a roughhouse. He was some sort of a boxing champion when he went to college back east, so I understand."

"It's J. K. Tolliver I'm after," Zack said. "I've got no bone to pick with Niles."

"Sure, sure," Hickok said. "By the way, how's the foot that Miss Smith stomped on?"

Zack took the bait. "So her name is Smith too," he said.

Hickok laughed. "Frank Niles wants to change it to Niles," he said.

Zack realized he had been trapped. "So what?" he snarled. He left the marshal's office and headed down Railroad Street, mumbling to himself. Why would he give a hoot if Frank Niles was sweet on the girl with the snapfinger eyes?

He began to understand that he was becoming sort of a marked man in Sioux Wells. Railroad men off shift were having a morning beer in some of the less pretentious saloons. Many of them were moving to doors and windows to watch as he passed by. Their interest was not actively hostile, but neither was it friendly.

Zack could hardly blame them. To them he represented another peril to their livelihoods. He was another burden on the already financially burdened Rocky. They had heard how Stan Durkin had stampeded the K-Bar-K herd. Although local courts might rule in favor of the Rocky the chances were that if the claim was carried higher, it probably would be allowed, along with the assessment of heavy legal costs. That might be the straw that would break the Rocky's back.

The morning westbound combination train would soon be due, and a gaggle of passengers were on the platform and sitting on the hard benches in the stuffy waiting room, along with the customary quota of idlers who were there to see a train come in.

Zack strode to the ticket booth, making sure everyone heard not only what he said, but the thud of his high-heeled boots.

"I want to see a fellow named Niles who seems to be the ramrod around here," he said. "Where does he hang out?"

The ticket agent, who was a thin man in an eyeshade and sleeveguards on the arms of his white shirt; almost swallowed his Adam's apple and acted as though he wanted to duck out of sight. He was forced to face it out, and pointed weakly toward a stairway that led to the second story. "Up there," he croaked. He fluttered around for a moment as though having the notion to leave the cage and race upstairs to warn his boss. But he decided against it, for Zack was already on his way to the stairs.

Zack mounted the steps and found himself in a hall that served several offices. Telegraph sounders clattered, and operators were busy at the keys. One room gave forth the inky odor of ledgers. Clerks were mounted on high stools laboring with pens on bills of lading.

The farthest door was closed, and its frosted glass panel bore the information that this was the office of Frank M. Niles, Division Superintendent.

Zack opened the door and entered. Frank Niles had a female secretary in the ante room. She was forty and plump, with china-blue eyes. Her eyes started to rove over Zack. Then she realized who he was, and she uttered a startled gasp.

"I came to see the boss," Zack said. The door to the inner office stood open and he could see Niles sitting at a big, varnished desk. He walked past the secretary into the inner sanctum.

Niles did not arise. "Well, well," he said crisply. "Do you always barge into business offices without being asked?"

Before Zack could answer, Niles arose, moved to the door and spoke to the secretary. "Jenny, I missed breakfast this morning. Would you mind going down to the Delmonico? Steak and eggs. Tell them to never mind those things they call potatoes. They fry them in coal oil. And just plain bread. I don't want toast burned to a cinder. A jug of black coffee."

The woman began arranging her hair and pinning on a bonnet. Niles closed the door, waited until sure she had left.

Then his manner changed. He smiled and extended a hand. Zack, surprised, accepted it.

"Good morning, Keech," Niles said. "You look healthy and fit. You had a strenuous introduction to Sioux Wells yesterday, but seem to have survived."

"Yeah," Zack said, baffled.

"We'll keep our voices down," Niles said. "I know why you're here, of course. I know because I was there when we got our orders from J. K. Tolliver."

"So this J. K. Tolliver really is here—in Sioux Wells?"

"Yes. That's between the two of us. The three of us, counting Hickok. Here's our plan. We want you to join these outlaws who have been robbing us."

"Join them?"

"Right. J. K. Tolliver is prepared to give you six thousand dollars if you break up this gang. The only way seems to be to get inside the gang itself."

"Why hasn't that been tried before?" Zack asked.

Niles picked up a cigar which lay smoking on an ash tray, revived the red glow and blew smoke reflectively as he considered his answer. "It has," he finally said. "With bad results, evidently. Hickok brought in a friend of his to attempt to get information on this outfit. He pretended to be a down-and-outer who swamped at the saloons for enough to live on in the hope of picking up information. He has disappeared."

"Disappeared. You mean he's run out?"

Niles shrugged. "We hope so. He was known as Jimmy Broom around the barrooms. Nobody has seen him for days."

There was silence for a time. "Before that," Niles went on, "we hired two experienced detectives for the same purpose. One was found dead, a knife in his back. The other quit and left Sioux Wells."

Zack could hear the telegraph instrument rattling faintly in the distance. Other sounds came from the bookkeeping room which was separated from Niles' office by a painted wooden wall. A door back of Niles' chair evidently led to a small inner office. The door was slightly ajar and Zack fancied he heard another faint sound from that direction.

"What makes you think I could swing a thing like this, even if I wanted to try?" Zack asked.

"You've got more in the pot. And more on the ball.

They were hired detectives. They had only their fees to lose."

"And their lives."

"Six thousand dollars is a nice sum," Niles said. "And J. K. Tolliver might be induced to sweeten the pot if things worked out."

Again Zack heard movement beyond the partly open door. He guessed the answer. J. K. Tolliver was there, in person, listening. That meant that he was in reality dealing directly with the president of the railroad and that Frank Niles was only acting as a mouthpiece.

Zack was caught on the horns of a dilemma. While six thousand dollars, if lost, would not cripple the K-Bar-K, there was the matter of his own pride. He had come to Sioux Wells to collect on the loss of the cattle, and his mission was public knowledge. J. K. Tolliver had cleverly placed him in a rather untenable position. He could throw up his hands and leave Sioux Wells admitting his defeat. Or he could follow his pride.

He raised his voice a trifle to make sure that whoever was listening could hear clearly. "I might try this," he said, "on one condition. The money is to be paid to Brandy Ben Keech, win or lose."

"What do you mean, win or lose?" Niles demanded.

"You know what I mean. From what you just told me these outlaws play for keeps. They've wrecked trains, murdered men. They tried to kill Hickok last night. They missed. They won't always miss."

"But that's the beauty of our plan," Niles said. "You're going to try to be one of them. An enemy of the Rocky."

"Beauty is the wrong word," Zack said. "Skunk might come closer to it. But you heard my terms. The Rocky pays my father, win or lose. I'll try to give them their money's worth. Being a spy sort of leaves a bad taste in me, but everything's fair in dealing with cutthroats."

Niles coughed, clearing his throat. "Pardon me a moment," he said. "I seem to be picking up a cold. I've got some tablets around somewhere."

He arose and entered the inner room, closing the door behind him. He returned after a few minutes. "I've thought it over," he said. "All right. Your father will be paid, win or lose—provided, of course, that we are satisfied that you have given us an honest effort."

Zack was sure beyond all doubt that Niles' superior was in the inner office and had given the word to go ahead. There could be many reasons why J. K. Tolliver did not want to appear in public in Sioux Wells, but the main one, no doubt, was that the railroad president did not want to become a target of the highbinders as Hickok had been.

Niles extended a hand. "It's a deal, then?"

Zack accepted it. Niles' grip was strong, very strong. He was a bigger man than Zack had believed. He was as tall as Zack himself and handled himself with the poise of a man who kept in trim and took pride in his physique. In spite of himself Zack was thinking of the Miss Smith with the snapping dark eyes. Only a strong man, educated, poised, such as Frank Niles, would interest a girl who had proved that she was no weakling herself the day she had drawn the derringer to back up her grandmother in the matter of the wounded antelope.

"Just how will we go about this?" Zack asked. "Any ideas as to the best way to weasel into the confidence of these train wreckers?"

"You've already made a good start at proving you've got no use for this railroad," Niles said. "I'd say your best path is to continue along that line. Convince everyone that you have every reason to hold a grudge against the Rocky."

"Build up a feud?"

"Exactly. We might add fuel to the flames right now. Everybody in town knows by this time that you came to my office this morning for a showdown. It's my bet that half of the town is waiting to see what happens. Let's give them a run for their money. What if this talk ended up in anger and threats of vengeance?"

Niles, not waiting for an answer, took the initiative. "And I tell you, sir, that I will not sit here and be threatened!" he shouted. "I must ask you to leave at once."

Zack got to his feet, taking his cue. "You'll be the sorriest man in Sioux Wells before I'm through with you, Niles," he thundered. "And so will the Rocky."

"I'm not armed!" Niles howled. "You wouldn't shoot an unarmed man, would you? If its a gunfight you want, I'm willing to oblige. I left my weapon at my home. Give me a chance to arm myself."

Zack thought this was carrying it a little too far. He kicked his chair against a wall with an impact that undoubtedly could be heard in the waiting room below. "No you don't, Niles," he said. "I want only the money that's coming to me. Don't try to fix it so that you can get some of your railroad gunmen to shoot me."

He stamped out of the office, slamming the door back of him. Jenny, the plump secretary, was just returning with a cloth-covered tray containing the breakfast Niles had ordered. Zack lifted the tray from her hands and hurled it against a wall.

Dishes shattered amid the debris of eggs and steak. Coffee streaked the wall and floor. Zack headed for the stairs with Jenny uttering weak moans of dismay. Niles shouted furious threats that were not all faked, for he was staring angrily at his ruined breakfast.

Descending the stairs to the waiting room, Zack found himself facing a lake of startled faces. He barged roughly among them, shouldering men aside. Reaching the outer platform, he was confronted by a different type.

Railroad men were gathering. Brawny brakemen,

switchmen, oilers, firemen, section hands. More men were leaving the repair shops at a distance and were racing to join the gathering. The word had spread. It occurred to Zack that it had spread too rapidly. It was as though the railroad's employees had expected that his talk with Niles would end in a declaration of war, and they were more than ready for it. Here was the man who had knocked out their champion, and they believed it had been a lucky punch. They were out to humiliate Zack, not only because of the raw wound to their pride, but because they were railroad men and Zack was a cowboy—an alien.

Zack found his path blocked by muscular men, some in greasy jumpers, some in the rough garb of section hands. "If'n he's a cowboy," someone shouted. "Let's see how he can ride. Fetch a crosstie, boys."

Howls of agreement arose. Men went racing off the platform to where a stack of crossties was stored. They lifted one of the ties and came hurrying back.

Zack moved to a wall, stood with his back against it. He had a hunch that all this had been planned beforehand—by Niles, no doubt, in order to add fuel to the appearance of a feud. But it was carrying the scheme too far. The mob meant business. It was being egged on by half a dozen loud-voiced, hard-eyed men who were heavily armed. Zack doubted if they were railroad men, although they wore striped caps and checked shirts. However, instead of brogans they had on high-heeled saddle-boots.

He had not drawn his six-shooter. He knew that to do so might change the situation. At the moment the members of the group were only in a mood to humiliate him. Bloodshed might change their temper and they would become a lynch mob.

Then he spotted Stan Durkin. The big, redheaded man, evidently no worse for wear, was standing at the back of the circle that ringed Zack in. He was taking no part in the taunting and profanity, but neither was he making any attempt to intervene

Zack singled him out. He lifted his voice so that he could be heard above the jeering. "Durkin! You, there! Your pals seem to think I was lucky yesterday. Maybe they'd like for you to have a second chance. I'm willing to give you another try."

Durkin straightened, bristling. Then he seemed to have a second thought. "I wouldn't want to rob the boys of their fun, cowpoke," he said. "They still want to see if you can ride a rail."

A new voice broke in. A feminine voice. "Surely, Mr. Durkin, you're not afraid of this Texas lout are you? You ought to be able to put him in his place without trouble, being as you're a railroad man."

The speaker was the comely Miss Smith. Apparently she had just entered the station from the door that faced on Railroad Street. She wore a neat, short-sleeved white dress and had a handbag dangling from an arm.

She also had command of the situation. She looked at the group that surrounded Zack. "Never let it be said that it takes twenty railroad men to lick one cowboy. It would be a blot on the honor of Sioux Wells forever."

Stan Durkin was palpably flattered at being singled out as a champion by such an attractive creature. He began to swell with importance and with the realization that he had a chance to redeem himself and quench his thirst for vengeance on Zack.

"Afraid!" Durkin roared scornfully, and came pushing through the group to face Zack. "Me, afraid of the likes of this saddle bum? He was lucky yesterday. Such luck can't last a second time. Put up your dukes, Texas."

Frank Niles descended the stairs from his office and joined the dark-haired girl. A self-satisfied smile tugged at the corners of Niles' mouth. That clinched Zack's belief that Niles had arranged this beforehand, even to the threat of the rail-riding. No doubt it was part of the scheme to build him up as a bitter foe of the railroad, but there were features of the confrontation that were puzzling. The majority of the men who were jeering him were railroad men, beyond question, but he could not shake off the belief that the real ringleaders were from a different stratum.

However, if it had been staged, Stan Durkin evidently had not been aware of it. He stood with fists poised in a boxing attitude before Zack. "This time I'm going to beat you to a froth," he promised. "Stand back, boys. Give me room to operate."

The group hastily moved back, forming a circle. Stan Durkin moved in on Zack. He was wary this time. Very wary. It was evident he hadn't forgotten the impact of the one blow Zack had landed the previous day. He began retreating, feinting, dancing aside, ducking. He was trying to lure Zack into making a rush, intending to trap him off balance.

Zack moved. He faked a rush and Durkin fell for it. Durkin jabbed eagerly with a long left, his right fist poised for a smash to the jaw. Zack let him start that intended knockout swing, let it whiz past harmlessly.

Then he swung his right. The same blow he had struck the previous day, on the same jaw. And with the same result.

Whack! Stan Durkin collapsed at the knees and pitched forward into Zack's arms to be lowered gently to the floor.

Zack looked around at the bystanders. Once again complete, unbelieving silence reigned.

The girl with the snapfinger eyes was the first to speak. "Holy cow!" she gasped. "Not again!"

Zack blew on his knuckles. "I don't believe we've ever been introduced, miss," he said. "I go by the name of Zachary Keech. From Round Butte, Texas. That's down in the Brazos River country."

He lifted his hat. "And you?" he asked.

"My name is Smith," she said. "Anita Smith. Congratulations seem to be in order again. And here's something else by which to remember me."

She lifted a slipper and once more stamped it down on his foot. Luckily it was the left foot this time. Zack's right foot was still tender from the event of the previous day.

Zack reeled to a wall, nursing the injured foot. "Miss, you *are* a hard loser," he mumbled.

"Indeed I am," she said grimly.

"I'll be careful in the future not to get within stompin' distance," Zack said. "Just why are you so down on Texas folks? Did someone from down our way do you dirt at one time or another?"

She started to answer that, then thought better of it. She turned away and took the arm of Frank Niles.

"My advice to you, Keech," Niles said, "is to take the next train out of town. There's nothing in Sioux Wells for you. Good day, sir."

He walked away with Anita Smith clinging to his arm.

Chapter 5

Men were bringing water and dousing it on Stan Durkin. Zack lingered until certain Durkin had suffered no serious injury. Then he left the depot, walking through the scattering drift of spectators who were now returning to their various pursuits. The ringleaders of the gathering had faded into the background.

The day was turning blazing hot again and Zack walked into the first saloon, moved to the bar and ordered a mug of beer. The barkeeper, who had entered just ahead of him after having been among the onlookers at the brief encounter in the depot, moved with haste to fill the order, so much so that he overfilled the mug, loosening a foaming Niagara across the bar top.

Other men came crowding into the place in Zack's wake, giving it the biggest rush of patronage at this hour of the day in its history. Zack, embarrassed, and trying to ignore it, was the center of all eyes, and most of those eyes were envious. One man even had the temerity to hurriedly place a hand on Zack's biceps. "What muscle!" the man said admiringly.

Others might have attempted the same thing, but a sudden hush came, a taut stillness. A new arrival had entered the saloon. A path magically opened for him.

The arrival was Wild Bill Hickok. The badge was pinned to a suspender. He stood at a short distance from Zack, staring with his sad eyes for a space. "Sunup," he said. "Be long gone from Sioux Wells come daylight tomorrow, Keech, or I'll be lookin' for you. Two fist-

59

fights, two insults to a lady, a try to have me killed and bein' mixed up in a hotel-room brawl all in twenty-four hours has tried my patience. Sunup."

Zack couldn't believe it. Hickok had been friendly to the point of fatherliness only a short time earlier. Now he was pronouncing that sentence that men had learned not to ignore. Deadline!

Zack felt the cold chill of the presence of sudden death. He could not understand this sudden change in the attitude of the marshal. He knew that men around them were suddenly crowding away to safer distance. He stood facing Hickok, still frozen by that inner knowledge that a wrong move might be his last.

Then he believed he understood. Once more it was all stage setting, melodramatic fakery. Like his feigned quarrel with Frank Niles this was to build him up further as an enemy of law and order—and of the railroad.

He turned away, pushed men aside, walked out of the saloon and headed down the sidewalk to the Traveler's Rest. Mounting to his room he unlocked the door, entered and locked the door back of him. The heat of the day gripped the room. He hung his hat on a peg, pulled off his boots and stretched out on the bed, trying to think.

He was confused. He was unable to decide where the stage play started and stopped and where he had faced reality. The threat of rail-riding had been very real. And his second encounter with Stan Durkin had not been prearranged. His aching wrist and hand assured him of that. His hand had taken real punishment.

He watched a fly make its erratic way across the ceiling. He was trying to decide whether to go through with this. By this time the K-Bar-K herd should be fifty or sixty miles up the trail—barring further obstacles such as the one that had got him involved with the Rocky Mountain Express. He was asking himself if he had not made a mistake in trying to force his claim on a railroad that already had deep trouble.

A hand tapped softly on the door, obviously being careful not to attract attention elsewhere. He got off the bed and lifted his six-shooter from the holster on the wall peg. "Who is it?" he called.

"Open," a muffled voice said. It was a feminine voice, and that voice belonged to the one who called herself Anita Smith. Zack hesitated. Anita Smith, if that was her real name, had proved that she was far from enthusiastic about his presence in Sioux Wells.

"Who's with you?" he demanded.

"Nobody. Open this door, you fool." That was Anita Smith, beyond a doubt. Headstrong, sassy.

He opened the door, still cautious. She pushed it wide open, sending him staggering. She slipped inside the room and locked the door while he regained his balance.

"You *are* very awkward, aren't you?" she commented. "And suspicious. Did you think I was bringing a posse to ride you on a rail?"

"Now I don't want to get into any fuss with you," Zack raged.

She lifted a warning finger to her lips. "Please speak softly. You are not bellowing at a herd of cattle. I have very good hearing. Furthermore, you know what it might do to my reputation if it became known I was here."

"How about my rep?" Zack replied. "And no stomping on my feet. I haven't even got boots on to protect me right now." In spite of himself he was obeying her warning to lower his voice so that it could not be heard beyond the door.

"My, my!" she said. "You do handle the language nicely. I thought all Texans talked like they had sand burs under their tongues."

Zack glared at her, but she did not wilt. "What do you want?" he demanded.

"Want? How fantastic. I only came here to give you some advice."

"Now that's mighty considerate of you," Zack said. "Of course, if I needed any such, you would be the very last person I'd apply to."

"Don't make rash statements," she said. "I came to tell you that, if you are smart, you should get out of Sioux Wells as fast as you can."

Zack eyed her for a long space in a silence during which he could hear the ticking of his watch which he had laid on the bureau.

"It seems like a lot of folks don't want me around here," he said. "First Hickok, then that Niles fella. Now you. It doesn't happen that all of you are interested in getting rid of me and that six-thousand-dollar claim I've got against the railroad?"

"Perhaps," she said. "But there could be other reasons."

He was remembering that he had seen Hickok coming from the suite occupied by Granny Smith and this girl the previous afternoon.

"How long have you called yourself by that name, Anita Smith?" he asked abruptly.

She arched her brows. "Why, everyone in Sioux Wells knows my name. Are you insinuating that I'm traveling under false colors?"

"I'm saying it out loud."

"And too loud," she murmured. "I came here to ask you to stay out of all this. Money isn't worth it. Six thousand dollars isn't worth your life."

"So that *is* it!" Zack said harshly. "It's the railroad that sent you to try to spook me. It was your fine friend, Frank Niles, who put you up to this, wasn't it? He only wants to get rid of me and my claim against his railroad. What will you get out of this?"

She glared at him, anger pushing a pink tide into her cheeks. "I sized you up as being intelligent, but you're only being pigheaded," she said. "Well, you've been warned. That's all I can do."

She turned, opening the door to leave. "Wait!" Zack exclaimed. "I want to know more about—?"

"About my private life?" she said. "About Frank Niles? That's none of your concern."

She was gone, closing the door after her.

He heard her move down the hall, heard the door of the suite at the front open and close. Then silence. He locked his door again and stretched out on the bed once more. He tried to figure out this new puzzle. The big question was: Who is this Anita Smith and what is her purpose in warning him to pick up his marbles and quit the game? She was a puzzle indeed. And so was her grandmother. Zack believed Anita Smith had not come here voluntarily. She had been sent by someone, and that someone might have been the wispy, gray-haired sharp-tongued grandmother.

He tried to look at it from every angle, including this new phase. There were a multitude of angles, it seemed, each with a sharp corner that could wound. Or even kill!

That thought aroused him. He gazed around and found that anyone peering from the tops of buildings that stretched ragged down Railroad Street from the hotel might have a view of him here in broad daylight.

He moved hastily to correct this, remembering the Ogallala Kid and Matt Pecos. And there was Stan Durkin, of course, who had reason to hold a real grudge against him, but Durkin, at the moment at least, could hardly be expected to be in shape to notch a fine sight on a target at that distance.

As he moved, the bullet came. It shattered glass in

the window. Much glass. The window was of the sash
type, with the lower half raised for ventilation. The bullet
tore through both panes, littering with glistening shards
both the floor and the bed where Zack had been re-
clining.

Zack crouched, snatching his six-shooter from the holster on the wall. He crawled to the window, peering.
The bright sun of early afternoon was in his eyes. The
sheet iron and tarpaper and shingled roofs of Sioux Wells
baked peacefully in the sun. What powder smoke there
might have been had been dissipated swiftly by the brisk
plains wind. What windows were in sight looked back at
him vacantly.

The shrill voice of a woman sounded. It was the large,
frizzle-haired woman, Gussie Bluebell, who had castigated
Ed Hake the time of the water tank shooting. She was
leaning from the windows of the Good Time.

"More trouble at the hotel!" she was screeching. "A
shootin' this time. Where's Hickok? Can't he keep law
an' order to this town? I declare, its' nothin' but fightin'
in the street, shootin' up water tanks an' brawls at the
hotel."

Footsteps came pounding to his door. Zack, careful to
stay out of line of fire through the window, turned the key
and opened the door. It was about the same group of
guests and loungers who had come up from the lobby as
had gathered here the day before. The same turkey-
necked desk clerk, who was also the owner.

Anita Smith also appeared, wide-eyed. She looked at
Zack and there was an I-told-you-so expression in her
face. She seemed greatly upset, and also thankful to find
him uninjured. With her was Julia Smith who looked
as though she had been interrupted at her knitting. In
fact, she still carried the knitting. There was one exception to this picture of peaceful demeanor. Zack was positive he saw Granny Smith conceal a weapon beneath

the knitting in her hands. It was a business-looking six-shooter.

"You again?" the hotel owner raged, staring aghast at the shattered glass. "How did this happen?"

"If you've got any notion that I shot them out just for fun, then get another notion," Zack said. "How in blazes do you think it happened? It wasn't done by kids throwing stones, you can take my word for that."

He moved to a wall, drew out his pocket-knife and dug a spent bullet from the plaster. "A .45," he said. "Not much help there. Half the population carries that gun."

"I'm asking you to leave my establishment," the hotel man thundered. He added hastily, "The cost for the windows will be two dollars."

Zack turned bleak eyes on the man. "In the first place, you miser, I doubt if fixing them will cost much more than half that. In the second place, I'm staying here until I decide to leave."

"That won't be any too soon," the man said. "At least I'll be rid of you before too many hours. I hear that Wild Bill has deadlined you. Even Hickok is tired of you and the brawls and shootings you've been in. And I want you to know that, as an honest Sioux Wells business man, you are less than welcome here."

"He's a saddle bum!" It was Granny Smith who spoke from the background. "Just a ruffian. I hear he even had the gall to threaten the superintendent of the railroad here about some foolish claim he is trying to press about a few cows he says were lost down the country."

Here it was again. The case of Zack Keech against the beneficent Rocky Mountain Express upon whose payrolls the majority of the population of Sioux Wells depended. Granny Julia Smith had drilled into a very live nerve with her interference in the discussion. Zack once more felt alone, facing the hostility of a community.

Once again it was Hickok who arrived and calmed

the angry waters. He looked at Zack with his pale, unreadable eyes, looked at the broken panes. "Did you see where the shot came from?" he asked.

"No," Zack said. "Maybe Gussie Bluebell did. She was the first to begin yowling."

"I'll talk to her," Hickok said. "Looks like I ought to shorten your stay in Sioux Wells. For your own sake if nothin' else. If you pulled out of town pronto, everybody might feel better about it. I mean pronto."

"I don't pronto very fast under these circumstances," Zack said. "Somebody just took a shot at me. Maybe he'll try again. That might give me a chance to drive a nail in his coffin."

Hickok shrugged. "Have it your way." He looked at the hotel owner. "Did I hear you tryin' to make this cowboy pay for these busted windows, Jud?" he asked. "Why?"

"I figger he shot 'em out himself," the man said. "Just to bring attention to him. He seems to like such."

"Now you know that ain't right, Jud Gregg," Hickok said mildly. "That bullet came from outside an' you know it. Otherwise the glass would have been scattered in the other direction. It's a case of damage at the hands of persons unknown an' you could hardly hold Keech responsible. I say to drop the subject."

"Just as you say, Marshal," Jud Gregg agreed hastily. "Just as you say."

"Otherwise, I'll run you in for makin' a false claim for damages," Hickok continued in his soft voice. "An' give you a boot under the coat tail in addition, for tryin' to take advantage of a guest in your hotel."

"I advise you not to skyline yourself while you arrange to leave town," he added, addressing Zack. "You've rubbed the fur of a lot of people the wrong way. Stay away from windows. Mind me now."

Hickok left, descending to the lobby. No sound came

back. Zack noticed with the annoyance of a man proud
of his own poise that the stairs, which squeaked un-
mercifully under the tread of himself and other persons,
gave forth no sound beneath Hickok's boots.

Jud Gregg left also, grumbling. The others drifted
away. Granny Smith and her deadly bundle of knitting
vanished into her quarters down the hall along with her
granddaughter, who gave Zack a glance back over her
shoulder—a glance that he believed bore concern for
him.

An Indian woman appeared with broom and dustpan
and swept up the broken glass. After she had left, Zack
moved the bed out of range of the window. He wedged a
chair under the doorknob to reinforce security, and
placed his pistol on the stand within reach.

He stretched out on the bed, trying to think. Suddenly,
he sat up and leaped from the bed. He moved to the
gouge in the plaster where the bullet had imbedded, and
lined it up with the approximate spot where the slug had
crashed through the panes of glass.

He stood rubbing his chin in perplexity. He had a
new problem to add to the rosary of problems over which
he kept mulling. The bullet had passed at least four
feet from him and a foot higher than his head. The
marksman could hardly have been that poor a shot, which
meant that he had made sure of missing by a wide
margin.

Zack resumed his recumbent position on the bed, trying to fit this new piece of the puzzle in with all the hectic
events that had dogged him almost from the moment he
had stepped off the train at Sioux Wells.

He did not know that he had fallen asleep until a
cooling breeze was moving through the empty frames of
the window. The sun had gone down and the first
lamps were being lighted in the town.

He was chagrined. "Somebody might have got in here

and cut your throat and you'd never have found it out," he told his reflection in the small mirror.

Inasmuch as he likely wouldn't have another chance to take advantage of the ultra-modern bathing facilities down the hall, he made his way there with towel and soap that he ordered from the flunky, and his razor. He had shaved that morning before going to court, but his dark beard was already roughening his lean jaws. Ordinarily he wouldn't have endured the nuisance of running a razor over his face twice in a day, but he went through the routine again and was very critical of the effect in the mirror above the washbasin, vaguely lighted by an oil lamp.

He showered, dressed and redid his string tie three times before he was partly satisfied with the result. He combed his thick hair with great care. He wouldn't admit to himself the real reason for all this extra grooming even while he was walking down the hall to the door at the front—the door back of which he expected to find the beautiful Anita Smith.

He was successful, up to that point. It was she who opened the door after he had finally steeled himself to tap on the panel. That had taken a little time. He had poised his knuckles four or five times above the panel, only to panic and stand motionless and perspiring a little as though some force had paralyzed his arm.

She stood looking at him with an inquiring smile. A cool, knowing, feminine smile. It came to him with freezing embarrassment that she must have been aware that he had stood there at the closed door for seconds, fighting the urge to retreat in disorder. A wise smile it was, the smile of one who was sure of herself and her power over him.

"Well, this *is* a surprise," she said. "Zachary Taylor is the name, I believe."

"Keech," Zach croaked. "Zachary Keech. Zachary Taylor was President a long ways back."

"Of course," she purred. "How could I have got it so wrong after the way you've turned this town upside down? You have become famous."

Zack waved that aside. He didn't want to talk about the past. He had removed his hat. He dropped it accidentally on the floor. He lunged to pick it up and butted his head against the door jamb. He straightened, beet-red. The girl was smiling coolly as though all this was only to be expected on his part.

"Can I do something for you?" she asked. "A cold, damp cloth on the head, perhaps? You might be developing a lump there."

Zack grinned. Somehow he felt suddenly at ease. "No bump," he said. "Skull's too thick. So's the brain."

Her smile changed. It matched a sudden intuitive feeling that between himself and this dazzling creature was an understanding.

"Affairs have been rather quiet with you lately, I imagine," she said. "It's been several hours since you've been shot at or have knocked out Stan Durkin. It must be monotonous. Are you here to try to stir up excitement?"

"Something like that," Zack said. "I likely will be stomped on again for being forward, not knowing you very well, but down in Texas we learn that if you don't throw your loop mighty quick and sudden, you'll never rope a steer."

"Or a heifer," she said.

Zack eyed her with growing respect. "Now, who'd ever guess that you'd know the difference."

"You'd be surprised at how many facts of life I'm acquainted with," she said. "Now, just what, or who, did you come here to catch in your loop?"

"I don't know what Sioux Wells has to offer in the way of eating places that would appeal to folks like you and your grandma," Zack said, "but I noticed one named the Delmonico that had the earmarks of being respectable and clean. I'm hoping that you and Mrs. Smith would do me the honor of having supper with me."

He saw that she was starting to refuse. "I promise not to get into any more trouble while I'm with you ladies, and will keep away from windows," he added hastily. "I imagine this place could serve up a beefsteak, or at least buffalo or antelope that might—"

Granny Smith's voice spoke from somewhere in the room. "Beef! That's my pick. Sticks to your ribs. I've had enough of buffalo hump and goat meat in my time."

Anita Smith hesitated. Zack believed the regret in her face was genuine. "I'm sorry," she said, "but we have a previous engagement for the evening."

Zack stood, fiddling with his hat. "Well, I missed," he said.

"Try again, sonny," Granny said, without appearing in person. Then she added as an afterthought, "Oh, I forgot. You won't be around long. I hear Bill Hickok has deadlined you."

"I'll be around until I decide to hit the trail on my own decision," Zack said.

"Good luck," Granny said. "You'll need it. 'Specially if you keep on tryin' to buck both Bill Hickok an' the Rocky. So long, sonny. Better to have loved and lost than never to have loved at all."

"Grandma!" the girl exclaimed, her composure fractured for the first time. "That's no way to talk."

"Heck, it was just a figure of speech," the invisible Granny snorted. "I don't put no stock in this love at first sight hocus-pocus. After all, you two only laid eyes on each other just lately, an' have been at sword's point ever since."

"For *goodness* sake, *will* you be quiet," her granddaughter demanded.

Zack found himself suddenly master of the situation and in a position to square up for several things, such as being stamped on. "I only came here to ask for company to supper," he said. "I didn't figure I was proposing marriage."

Anita Smith glared at him, her lips tightening. "Well, I never!" she exploded. "You *are* a barbarian, aren't you?"

Zack backed out of reach. "I don't aim to have another toe mashed," he said. "I'll say good evening, ladies. I hope I have better luck next time."

He turned away and Anita Smith slammed the door shut. Faint words came from beyond the panel. He knew she and Granny were engaged in heated talk, but he did not linger to attempt to eavesdrop.

He made his way down the hall toward the stairs that led to the lobby. As he reached it he encountered a man who was ascending. The arrival was Frank Niles. He wore a natty dark cutaway coat and trousers that matched the derby that was perched on his head. A polka-dot cravat carried a pearl stickpin. He bore the fresh aroma of barber's bay rum and hair oil.

Zack could not explain why he took the next step. It was perhaps because he understood that Frank Niles was arriving to escort Anita Smith and probably Granny out to supper. This was the previous engagement she had mentioned, no doubt.

He grasped Niles' derby by its curled brim and jammed it down over its wearer's ears. For an instant both he and Niles were stunned by this unexpected turn of events.

Then Niles, with a snarl of fury, wrenched the ruined derby from his head. "Why you . . . !" he frothed.

He started swinging with both fists. This was not play-acting as part of the plan to build up the feigned feud between Zack and the railroad company. This was the real thing.

Zack weathered that first flurry, but was forced to

come to close quarters. Wedged on the narrow stairway between the rail and the wall they could do little but claw and maul at each other for a moment. Niles teetered back, losing his balance. He grasped Zack's arms as he fell and carried him along as he plunged backward down the stairs, the two of them rolling over and over.

The stairs stood up under the punishment and they reached the floor of the lobby with Zack underneath. Niles rammed a knee into his stomach, driving from him what little breath he had left. He retaliated by managing a left uppercut with his only free arm to Niles' throat. That caused Niles to weaken enough for him to twist free.

They got to their feet and went at each other with the primal ferocity of two evenly matched males who were not too sure what they were fighting over, except that they had known from the first moment they met that they had little use for each other and now was the time to prove their dislike.

Three or four of the customary idlers had occupied the two rocking chairs and the sofa in the lobby. They scattered like quail as the avalanche descended and the two antagonists came battling among them. One, too slow to escape, fell, and avoided being trampled underfoot only by rolling and crawling free, squeaking in terror.

Hotel manager Jud Gregg, horror-stricken, came timorously from the shelter of his counter. "Stop it!" he quavered. "Stop it this instant! You're wrecking—"

It ended in a groan as the two men, swinging wildly at close quarters, fell over one of the rocking chairs. The chair disintegrated.

Niles seized up a rocker to which clung one of the legs and attempted to bring it down on Zack's head. The unwieldy weapon missed, and Zack landed a short right to the body—the same right that had twice leveled Stan Durkin. But it lacked steam after these hectic moments of supreme activity. However, the blow still had enough authority to drive Niles staggering back against the counter which Jud Gregg had just deserted.

The counter toppled. The ledger, which contained the names of guests, fell amid the clatter of pens, inkstands and handbills. Jud Gregg uttered another moan of horror. "Stop it!" he wept.

Niles picked up the ink bottle, which was a hefty object made of glass, and hurled it at Zack. Zack ducked and the bottle shattered one of the large front window panes. Ink was splattered over the ceiling and walls. Jud Gregg covered his eyes.

"Someone get Hickok!" he implored.

A gunshot roared in the room. Dust gusted up from the floor near the feet of the struggling men. "You fools!" an authoritative voice snapped. "Stop it, before I put a slug where it'll hurt."

Zack and Niles quit a combat that had reached the point of futility, due to sheer exhaustion. Gunplay was not in the mind of either man. What they sought was physical victory. Zack was beginning to feel utterly foolish for having started this. He was entirely to blame. He admitted that. No self-respecting man would have reacted any other way than had Niles to the affront.

He backed away from Niles. He discovered that the gunshot had not come from Wild Bill Hickok. There was no sign of Hickok. The street windows were lined with pop-eyed citizens, peering into the lobby. The stairs were packed with spectators who had come from the guest rooms or by way of the rear outer stairs.

In the forefront of the group on the stairs stood Granny Julia Smith. She held in her hand a wicked-looking, snub-nosed pistol. The powder smoke from the shot was still coiling up the stairway.

"What in blue blazes started all this?" she demanded.

"This fellow insulted me," Frank Niles panted. "He's

been asking for trouble with me because I'm in charge of the railroad's business here."

Blood dripped from Niles' nose, staining his fine garb. One sleeve of his tailored coat was ripped. His hair was matted with perspiration and gore, some of which had come from Zack who had a gashed cheekbone and other bruises.

Niles said to Zack, "I'll kill you the next time."

There was ferocity in the man, a cold savagery that appalled Zack, and brought him up alert and ready for anything.

Hickok arrived, jostling spectators aside and forcing his way into the lobby. He looked at Niles. "My God, Frank!"

He turned to Zack. He lifted his eyes upward as though appealing to a higher power. "All right," he said in a strained voice. "This will cost you fifty dollars tomorrow, not to mention maybe thirty days working on the road gang. There'll be damages to this hotel in addition."

"Sorry, Marshal," Zack said. "As I recall it, you told me to dust out of here before sunup."

"I'll see to it that you stay a little longer," Hickok said. "Who started this?"

"I did," Zack said.

"Naturally," Hickok sighed. "How and why?"

"I didn't like the way his hat fitted him. He sort of resented it, and that's how it went."

"Is that all there was to it, Frank?" Hickok demanded.

"There's a little more to it than that," Niles said. "He made threats this morning when he came to my office and demanded that I fork over a lot of money for some cattle that he claims were killed because of the railroad. He admitted that not one cow was hit by our rolling stock and that they died in a stampede which he claims was caused by one of our trains. He ignored the fact that the cattle should not have been held so near our right-of-way. It's my guess they were held there deliberately, just so they could put in a false claim against us."

"They were there because we couldn't prod them into crossing your blasted track," Zack said.

Granny Julia Smith intervened. "Better go see a saw-bones and get that cut on your face taken care of, cow-poke," she said. "Looks like it needs some stitchin'. As for you, Mr. Niles, I think me an' my granddaughter can take care of that nose. It don't look like it's busted. Come with us. I've got medicine an' court plaster."

"I'll go along with you," Hickok said to Zack. "It looks like I better keep a closer eye on you. I never saw anybody what could get into more trouble in a hurry. Now you've about wrecked a hotel."

"Who's goin' to pay for this?" Jud Gregg howled. "Look at this lobby, Marshal! That window alone will cost ten dollars, if a cent. Two busted chairs. My counter wrecked, papers scattered and tromped on. Who's—?"

"You'll be paid, Jud," Hickok said. "Quit yowlin'."

Hickok led Zack out of the Traveler's Rest and headed down the sidewalk. Once they were out of hearing of others, the marshal snarled, "You sort of overdid it, cow-boy. You really didn't have to pick a brawl with Frank Niles to prove your point did you?"

"Point?"

Hickok glared at him. "Have you forgot you can get your cattle money by trying to get the goods on these highbinders? You've already made yourself unpopular enough with railroad people without pickin' a fight with Niles. You tried to make his face over. Niles is on our side. Your side."

Zack was holding a handkerchief to his dripping injury. "He's a lot tougher man than Stan Durkin," he commented. "Fact is I was mighty glad when that old lady interfered. I wonder who she is? I've seen trail bosses that were milk and water compared to her. Did you see that gun she fired? You'd be surprised at other things I happen to know about her."

"Nothin' would surprise me from now on," Hickok said. "Here's Doc Appleton's office. It's unlocked. Likely he's over at the Ox Yoke, playin' monte. I'll round him up."

"Why did you fake that shot at me in my room this afternoon?" Zack asked.

Hickok smiled. "So you knew it was me? I just wanted to find out somethin'."

"And did you?"

"Maybe. Most people, if they had any sense, would have cleared out of town after bein' shot at, or been jumped with clubs like you've been. I wanted to know if you'd stampede."

Hickok walked away then. Zack waited in the doctor's office until the marshal returned with the pudgy, bulbous-nosed medic who was testy at being called away from the monte table.

Zack, his injuries doctored and court plastered, paid the two-dollar fee and left with Hickok. "I'll see you in court in the mornin'," the marshal said.

"I thought you might throw me in jail," Zack said.

"Jail's full. If I was you, I'd spend the evenin' at the Good Time."

"The Good Time? That'd be the last place I'd want—"

"For what you've got in mind, I figure that's a fine place to hang around tonight," Hickok said.

"I see," Zack answered. Reluctantly, he took the marshal's advice and headed for the bawdy music hall alone.

Chapter 6

The Good Time was attempting to live up to its name. A four-piece band consisting of a trumpeter, a clarinet, a drummer and an ump-ah tuba, came to life occasionally and beat out deafening sounds that went for music. Now and then a girl in tights offered song and dance numbers on a small stage set at an angle in a corner. A tiny dance floor was available for those who bought tickets for the privilege of struggling around the enclosure with one of the girls. Between times a mechanical piano kept the pace going.

The Good Time was busy. It was a large wooden structure with tinsel hanging from the beams, and posts bearing advertisement from breweries and distilleries.

Zack bought a mug of beer at the bar. The beer was pleasingly cold. "We git ice by the carload from Omaha, mister," a barkeeper informed him. "This here is the classiest emporium between Chicago an' Frisco, if you ask me, an' I've seen 'em all."

Zack carried his mug to a table that had just gone vacant, and at which there was no gambling and took one of the chairs. He expected company, which was the rule in places like this, and he did not have to wait long. Also, as he had expected, the company was feminine. His uninvited table companion was the buxom, peroxide blonde whose head he had seen at a window above the day of the water tank episode.

"Howdy, cowboy," she said in a graveled voice as she gave him a slap on the shoulder and seated herself in the nearest chair which she hitched closer. "What name do you go by?"

"Captain Kidd," Zack said. "And you?"

She threw back her head and laughed loudly. "I happen to know different," she said. "You've made a rep for yourself here in Sioux Wells in the last couple of days. Keech is your name and everybody in town knows it. As for me, you can call me Gussie."

"Gussie Bluebell?"

"You know me, cowboy? Now, I can't recall—"

"I was around when a buffalo hunter baptized you with a bullet through a water tank," Zack said. "Something tells me that was your first baptism."

Gussie Bluebell again threw back her head and shook the room with great laughter. She slapped him once more on the back. "So we're old acquaintances," she roared. She beckoned another girl who had been hovering close. "Two, Mabel," she said. "Old Kentucky straight. The best is none too good for this man here."

The drinks were brought.

"Here's to sin and the devil," she said, holding aloft her glass. "And to the Rocky Mountain Express. I hear they've kicked you around some."

Zack hesitated. Gussie Bluebell's bluff, coarse manner did not ring exactly true. Beneath the powder, rouge and peroxide she seemed to be a woman of forty, marked by lines of care rather than dissipation. He felt that she was studying him beneath that hail-fellow manner as though asking herself an urgent question.

"I'll drink to that," he said. He noticed that she barely touched the glass with her lips. She again pounded him on the shoulder, spilling the contents of her glass into the sawdust, apparently accidentally. "You look like my kind of man, cowboy," she said.

Then a cool, authoritative voice said, "Hello, Texas man. Good evening, Gussie."

Gussie was replaced at the table so swiftly and expertly that Zack blinked. Evidently Gussie knew better than to protest, for she moved away to give her attention to other patrons.

The new arrival was neither coarse-voiced, blonde nor dressed in spangles. She was good-looking, very much so and was considerably younger than Gussie, but still mature. She had coppery-red hair, very straight lips and green-flecked eyes. She had character—the character of a diamond. Wise, sophisticated, hard.

"Hello, Mr. Keech," she said. "Oh, yes, I know your name. You've become famous in the Wells lately. My name is Lila. Do you want another drink?"

"Lila what?" Zack said. "Let me guess. Lila Lilac? Or Lila Hyacinth. Or maybe Lila—"

"Any will do," she said, smiling. "To you, I'm just Lila. That's good enough, at least for now."

"Meaning our long friendship might not last?"

"I hope not. How about that drink?"

"I have a feeling I better keep my wits about me tonight," Zack said. "Are you Gussie's daughter, by any chance?"

She laughed. "Better not let Gussie hear a remark like that. She's not that old. Besides, she works for me."

"Works for you?"

"It happens that I own the Good Time," she said. "This is how I make my living." She saw him admiring the dark evening dress that she wore. It was rich and expensive in contrast to the tinseled, knee-length costumes the percentage girls had on. "It isn't too bad a living," she added. "But I want to do better."

Zack understood that he had been dropped a cue. "We all do," he said.

It *had* been a cue, and he apparently had given the right answer. "It's so noisy here," she said. "We can talk in my office without having to shout."

She arose and led the way down the length of the room through a rear door. Zack was aware that many curious eyes followed them, and some were envious. To the left was a small stage and a girl in tights was standing there awaiting the rise of the curtain to begin her song-and-dance number.

A stairway led to the second floor, and there was a rear door that evidently opened into the outdoors. Lila unlocked a door to the right which had painted on it the word Private.

It turned out to be a business office—and just that. A closed roll-top desk, filing cabinets and a slanting bookkeeping table with its high stool occupied the major part of the wall space. There were swivel chairs with worn leather cushions, cuspidors, a table bearing ash trays and a large iron safe. The floor was covered with faded green carpet. The stubs of cigars lay in the ash trays and the room carried the reek of recent smoking. Zack noticed the band on one of the half-smoked cigars that proclaimed it as an expensive make.

Lila had a twinkle in her eye as she watched him take in the drab surroundings. She seated herself at the closed desk and motioned him to take one of the swivel chairs. "You seem to have expected something else," she said. "This is really my office. I don't live at the Good Time."

Zack grinned. "I'm doubly glad I didn't take that second drink. Something tells me this is not a social event."

She glanced toward the door, making sure it was tightly closed. "We can talk freely here," she said. "The walls are padded with straw and double to kill sound. Even so, it will be best to keep our voices down."

"Seems like I've heard that before somewhere," Zack said. "Doesn't anybody trust anybody in this town?"

"Where did you hear it?"

"A little bird told me. What's the subject for tonight's discussion?"

"I understand you've had no luck with trying to squeeze money out of the Rocky," she said.

"None so far," Zack replied.

"Maybe you're not using the right approach."

Zack delayed his answer, trying to choose the right words. There was humming excitement within him. He was sure now what this was all about and why Hickok had advised him to spend his evening at the Good Time. The honky-tonk was apparently an important link in the outlaw organization, and this cool, handsome young woman might even be its head.

Their eyes met. She nodded. "You want money from the Rocky," she said. "I want money too. So do some of my friends. We intend to get it."

Zack debated whether to feel his way, or to rush in. He took the plunge and rushed. "From what I hear, some folks have already been cashing in pretty good."

"The hard way," she said. "Freight car robbing is hardscrabble, penny-ante stuff compared to other ways. Ladies underwear and washing machines and truck like that eat up all the profits peddling them."

Zack was of a notion to mention that stealing forty thousand dollars' worth of gold dust hardly could be listed as penny-ante profit, but decided against it.

She suddenly arose, moved to his side and kissed him. "That's only to seal the deal," she said.

She moved to the door, opened it and called a name so softly Zack could not catch it. Footsteps approached, and she ushered in a man. He was burly, garbed in the dungarees, striped cap and blue shirt of a railroad worker —with exceptions. He wore cowboots and carried a brace of six-shooters in holsters. His eyes were smoky dark, wise, without warmth. Zack remembered him. He had been the ringleader in the rail-riding demand at the depot the previous day.

"This is Jim Axel," she said. "The Ax. You'll enjoy knowing him better."

Zack doubted that. There was nothing particularly friendly in the inspection The Ax was making of him. The man finally shrugged, and said, "Come on, Keech."

Zack debated it. Prudence told him that he was wading into waters whose depth was unknown. Black waters. But, within him was a stubbornness, a humming anger at the arrogance of these people who were taking it for granted that he would do their bidding.

He made his decision and moved to leave the room with the swarthy man. Lila spoke. "One thing," she said. "From this point on, tall man, there is no turning back. Let that be understood."

Zack looked at her. "For either of us," he said.

The Ax led the way out of the Good Time by way of a rear door that avoided parading through the main gambling room before the eyes of patrons. They emerged into starlight. A prairie wagon, its weathered canvas tilt sagging drunkenly over the bows, stood nearby. A four-horse team stood in harness, the animals drowsily slapping at mosquitos with tails and twitching manes A bearded driver lolled on the seat, the reins wrapped around the whipstock. In the darkness, all that Zack could make out about the man was that he was garbed as a freighter. Like The Ax, he was heavily armed.

"We're goin' for a ride," The Ax said. He parted the ragged curtain that hung over the rear bow, and motioned for Zack to mount.

At that moment a commotion arose in the distance. The sounds came from the direction of the depot, which was not far from their position. "Git Hickok!" someone was shouting. "Fetch the marshal an' the coroner! My God! You ought to see *this!*"

"Let's take a look," Zack said. The Ax started to protest, but Zack was already on his way, and the man had no alternative but to follow. Zack walked to the street along a passageway between the Good Time and a neighboring building. Men were pouring from the music hall, and other citizens were passing by on the run, heading for the depot. Zack followed them. Hickok passed him, moving in long strides, and reached the scene ahead of him. He shouldered through the increasing press of onlookers.

A single night lamp in the waiting room gave light through the dingy windows. That vagueness was a blessing, hiding some of the horror of what lay at the feet of the staring arrivals.

Zack went cold to the marrow. It was the body of a man. He had been tortured. His body was naked, and the scars of the ordeal he had endured were ghastly visible.

"Injuns!" someone croaked.

Hickok knelt by the body and removed a paper that had been hung by a thong around the victim's neck. On it was a message printed in big letters:

HICKOK HERE'S YOUR SPY

"Not Indians," Hickok said. "White men."

His eyes lifted. The one he singled out was Zack. Then, quickly, the marshal turned away. But Zack had got the warning. Beyond a doubt, this was the missing man, known as Jimmy Broom, whom Hickok had brought in to attempt to get evidence against the train thieves.

Hickok had said that Jimmy Broom was his personal friend. Jimmy Broom had not died easily. There was no expression in the marshal's lined face, but he had the capacity for curbing his emotions, veiling them from public gaze.

"Who is he?" someone in the crowd asked.

Hickok did not respond, but the information was supplied by other bystanders. "He's been hangin' around town lately," someone volunteered. "A month or so. Ain't he the one that showed up, busted, an' lived on what money he could pick up out of the sawdust by swampin' an' sweepin' out at the Good Time? They called him Jimmy Broom, fer he always had a broom in his hand."

Zack saw that The Ax was drifting out of the circle. The Ax looked in his direction, and that was an order to follow. Zack hesitated, then left the group, acting as though he had seen enough of this horror. The Ax was ahead of him, and both drifted off the sidewalk into the darkness between buildings and returned to the wait-ing prairie wagon. Zack was remembering Lila's words that once he went with The Ax there would be no turning back. That would be doubly true, he realized, if he entered the wagon for the ride The Ax had mentioned.

Without a word he climbed into the interior of the wagon. The Ax joined him, the driver kicked the brake loose, spoke to the horses and the vehicle lurched into motion.

There were packing boxes aboard that served as seats. Zack tried one, but preferred to sit on the floor, wedging himself into place as best he could as the springless wagon jolted over rough going.

The Ax managed to roll a cigarette and get it lighted. The flare of the match accented the sardonic look on his tough face. His hair jutted like crow's wings from be-neath the brim of his hat.

The wagon lurched ahead. The rear curtains swayed open with the motion of the vehicle, giving fleeting glimpses of their route. The wagon was following a traveled road southward out of Sioux Wells. It paralleled the railroad yards for a time, then swung away from the tracks. The Ax, who had chosen to place himself near the rear bow, seemed particularly interested in some object outside. Zack peered. What The Ax was looking at was a single railroad car that stood alone on a remote sidetrack, well removed from the clutter of boxcars and gondolas that cluttered the yards they were leaving.

The Ax became aware that Zack was gazing also. "Damned rich bugs," he growled. "Ride on velvet an' eat off gold plate while the likes of me sit in a stinkin' hide wagon."

Zack saw that the car glistened with varnish, and its platforms and windows were trimmed in polished brass. It was dark and silent, but he could see fine curtains at the windows.

"Who?" he asked.

"J. K. Tolliver, that's who," The Ax said. "It's the Tolliver private car. It's been settin' there for a month, waitin' fer his majesty to find time to use it. They say it cost a pretty penny to build."

"But I understood that the Rocky is scratching bottom," Zack said. "If they can afford a car like that they can afford to pay what they owe me."

"They'll pay you an' everybody else before this is over," The Ax promised.

The glittering palace car and the lights of Sioux Wells faded back of them as the wagon creaked along the wheeltrack that wound through the sea of buffalo grass which clung tightly to the earth, still hot from the day's sun. A pair of coyotes, sounding like a pack, lamented their passing with weird, shrilling chorus. The driver, on one occasion, aroused and said, "Bufflers! Half a dozen of 'em. They're gittin' scarce in these parts. I'll come back tomorrow an' git me some horns an' hides."

Zack began to doze. One thing he could tell The Ax for sure. J. K. Tolliver was already in Sioux Wells, secretly and under another name to avoid persons like Zack who were pressing claims, or creditors clamoring for money from the railroad.

He had been maneuvered into this by the invisible J. K. Tolliver in the hope of saving the Rocky Mountain

Express from bankruptcy. He was also being led by a Delilah who called herself Lila into pretending that he was joining the Rocky's enemies. He was being used by both sides. He was sure that it had all been too easy—this being invited to join the outlaws. They were either giving him rope to hang himself and suffer the same fate as had Jimmy Broom, or were using him for some other purpose he could not imagine.

He only knew that The Ax distrusted him, and would kill him, no doubt, if he made a wrong move. Lila probably would do the same. She posed as an important person in the outlaw setup, perhaps its head. He wondered if that were true. As for J. K. Tolliver, that individual was risking only money. And then there was William Butler Hickok. Zack was not sure just where the marshal stood in this arrangement. He had come stampeding into Sioux Wells to do battle with the Rocky Mountain Express, and now he was riding to some sort of a rendezvous with the outlaws who were preying on the railroad. The maneuvering had been done mainly by Wild Bill. It was Hickok who had talked him into trying to pull the Rocky's chestnuts out of the fire. It was Hickok who had dangled the six-thousand-dollar bait in front of him.

Then there were two persons named Smith who fitted into this somewhere, he was sure. But where? Grandma Julia and her gorgeous granddaughter were sailing under false colors. He was also sure of that. Were they working with the highbinders also?

The wagon jolted on hour after hour through the night. Zack tried to sleep, but failed. He had too many perplexing problems that kept rearing up, nagging him. He believed The Ax dozed occasionally. At times the driver would arouse to remind loafing horses that he held a whip or to curse chuckholes and condemn all prairie dogs to perdition.

The thud of hoofs became audible. The Ax awakened completely, but after a moment or two settled back with a grunt of disinterest. At least three riders overtook the wagon and moved ahead, but they swerved off the trail, giving the vehicle a wide berth. There was no reaction at all from The Ax or the driver. It was as though this had been expected. Zack caught only a vague glimpse through the rear curtain of the riders in the starlight. He had the impression that one wore a slicker and was small. A woman, perhaps.

The wagon rolled onward. The trail carried them up-grade for miles out of the rich river basin and to the dryer, buffalo-grass plains. From far away came the lonely wailing of a train whistle. Such a sound could carry for miles in this stillness.

Dawn was at hand when they reached their destination. The fragrance of newly cut hay and running water was in the air. The horses quickened their pace, eager to be free of the harness.

Buildings loomed up and took form as the roofs and walls of a ranch spread. Someone outside said grumpily, "A hell of a time fer everybody to pull in. I'll help with the hoss's, Simmons."

There was an oath. "No names, you fool!" The Ax snarled, leaping from the wagon. "Next time, you'll regret it."

"We're here," he said to Zack. "We'll find some cawfee an' a bait of grub, then I'll locate a bunk fer you."

Zack alighted from the wagon. The layout straggled across a flat between swells in the plain. There was a rickety pole corral, a slab-sided wagon shed, a squatty house with weather-boarded sides that had never been painted. A huge haybarn dominated the spread. On the flats beyond he made out the shape of half a dozen sizable haystacks. This was new country, but this ranch already seemed defeated, its buildings weathering into the darkness of the land. A windmill creaked, and Zack heard the throb of the valve stroke as water was being pumped into the hayfields.

"This way," The Ax said. Zack followed him toward the house where lamplight showed. Back of him he heard the rattle of chains on the swingles and the creak of harness as the driver and the grumbling man freed the horses and led them away.

They mounted patched steps to a crooked stoop. The door was opened by someone inside. Zack followed The Ax into what turned out to be the kitchen, and found himself facing the steely-handsome girl from the Good Time—Lila.

"Good evening, Keech," Lila said calmly. "Or good morning, rather. Did you enjoy the trip?" Before Zack could answer, she continued, "I was one of the riders who passed the wagon down the trail. I couldn't get away from the Good Time until after you and Axel were well on your way."

She was sitting at a table, a cup containing coffee in her hand. Two other men also were at the table, which was long and built of solid planks, flanked by wooden benches. The table would take care of more than a dozen at one seating. Zack began to realize that this house, which appeared so small and dilapidated from the outside, was surprisingly big and not at all shoddy in furnishings or comfort.

"Welcome to Box Springs Ranch," Lila said. "You'll find this a very interesting place. This gentleman with the coffee dripping from his mustache is Jerry. The other one is Kerry. As a matter of fact, we don't worry about names. We only use them for the sake of convenience. We *do* put much stock in action."

Lila's companions were garbed similarly to The Ax, but they were no more railroad workers than was he. And just as hard-eyed and just as heavily armed.

"When do we begin this action?" Zack asked.

Lila smiled and looked at her companions. "Now that's what we like, isn't it, boys? A man of action. Of course, he's already proved that. I didn't see it with my own eyes, but he knocked out Stan Durkin with a single punch. To prove it was no accident he did it again. And he fought a pretty rough brawl with Frank Niles."

"Niles?" one of the men said, and eyed Zack with increased interest. "The big augur of the Rocky? How did it come out?"

"He found Niles tougher and faster with his fists than Stan Durkin, so I understand," Lila said.

She smiled at Zack. "It's time you got some sleep. Axel will show you to a bunk. As for action, my friend, you'll soon find some. Get plenty of sleep. You're likely to need it. But, first, have some grub and coffee."

Chapter 7

The Ax led Zack out of the house and across the ranch yard to the huge haybarn. The structure looked as though it might collapse at any moment under the weight of the wild hay in the loft.

Once they were inside the building The Ax lighted a lantern and Zack discovered that, like the ranch house, the outer appearance of neglect was a deception. The barn was braced strongly inside with beams and supports.

The Ax opened a trap door and they descended a steep stairway into a sizable dugout beneath the structure. This was a hidden sleeping quarters and there were half a dozen bunks in the place, with four occupied by sleepers who began stirring and mumbling profane objections to being awakened at this hour.

"Here's yours," The Ax said, indicating an empty bunk. "Help yourself to whatever you need. There's plenty to pick from."

He swung the lantern around so that Zack could see that the dugout was piled high with an astounding assortment. There were mattresses, pillows, sheets, blankets.

"Take yore pick," The Ax said grinning. "Ever sleep on a silk sheet? Here's yore chance. Sleep like a king fer once. When you git tired of them jest throw 'em away an' git new ones."

This was loot from Rocky Mountain Express trains. A wealth of it. Zack hesitated, then selected bedding and made up the bunk while The Ax waited with the lantern.

"Good night," The Ax said. "Sleep good. There won't be anythin' doin' all day."

He mounted the steps and the trap door dropped in place back of him. Daylight had strengthened enough so that wan light filtered into the dugout through cracks in the floor. Zack settled down on the bunk. He had plenty of time to think, for sleep eluded him. The other occupants of the hideout finished their interrupted rest, dressed and left by way of the trap door before he became drowsy.

He could hear the muted sounds of activity. Dogs yammered and squabbled somewhere, evidently in kennels. Pans and dishes rattled and he caught the fragrance of bacon being cooked. Horses whickered somewhere.

Then he slept. It was past noon when he awakened. The other bunks were still empty. He suspected that someone had been left on watch over him, for The Ax returned and lighted a lamp that stood in a bracket attached to a post.

Zack dressed. He got a better look at the wealth of loot in the place. Along with the bedding there were crates of clothing, boots, shirts, underwear, trousers, hats.

"Help yourself," The Ax said. "If you ride with us, you dress in the best. It's all paid for by the Rocky. An' we can furnish the top in the way of saddles, guns an' such. Hair tonic, razors, bay rum. We got it. Just ask. An' firewater."

"Santa Claus?" Zack asked.

The Ax's broad, hard face cracked into a crooked smile. "You guessed it. You can wash up at the trough outside. You'll find razors, soap an' towels. We picked a thousand razors in one day off a razor tree."

"A tree named the Rocky Mountain Express," Zack said.

"The market wasn't ripe for sellin' razors at that time," The Ax said, "so we was stuck with 'em."

Zack gazed around at the wealth of offerings, particularly the clothing. "A man could make a dude out of himself in this place, so much so he'd spend most of his time admiring his shadow," he said. He looked down at his own garb and shrugged, making no offer to array himself in the more expensive displays.

The Ax was watching him without expression, but he suddenly knew he had made a mistake. He hadn't been able to bring himself to wear stolen property. His instincts were all against it. Brandy Ben Keech had always hewed strictly to the line of honesty, and it had become a part of Zack's code. He sensed that somewhere in the book The Ax was keeping on him a demerit had been placed.

He and The Ax mounted to the floor of the barn. A few pieces of wheeled equipment, rakes, harrows and a mowing machine that needed repair stood in the place. He wondered what additional loot was hidden under the hay in the loft.

Emerging into the ranch yard through the double wagon doors that sagged on rusty strap hinges, Zack saw before him a scene commonplace on the plains where ranchers and dirt farmers bet the government they could defeat time and the weather and the loneliness by acquiring land.

A man in bib overalls and ragged straw hat was working on the windmill while a mowing machine with a team of horses stood idle nearby. A slovenly woman in calico and sunbonnet was listlessly hanging out a washing on a line back of the house. A few cattle and horses dotted a pasture beyond the haystacks which were enclosed by high barbed wire.

A man appeared amid the haystacks and left the enclosure by way of a gate which he was careful to chain tightly shut. Zack could have sworn that the man had emerged from one of the stacks itself. He looked at The

Ax who scowled. "See nothin', say nothin', hear nothin'," The Ax warned.

The haystacks, no doubt, were false fronts, like the ramshackle appearance of the house and barn, serving as hideouts for members of the outlaw organization and likely also as storehouses for loot.

Zack was served food by the slovenly dressed woman who, on closer look, turned out to be much younger and more active than she had seemed at a distance. The slovenliness and the washing were part of the plan to represent Box Springs Ranch as not worth attention.

The woman, like Lila, was hardened by life. She also liked the attention of any males around, for she brightened when Zack appeared and moved around, skirt hem swinging as she fried steak and eggs and potatoes, and heated coffee in a pot. It was a solid, satisfying meal.

"We had fresh oysters from Chesapeake Bay, an' terrapin soup a couple weeks ago," she said. "But we run out of all that stuff. It was meant for some miner who had hit it rich in the diggin's, an' was tryin' to make a splash." She fluttered her eyelashes at Zack. "I'm Anna May," she added.

"And I'm the Queen of Sheba," Lila spoke, entering the kitchen. "Throw out that sludge you call coffee and make some fresh in the small pot. I need something to wake me up and not to shatter my nerves."

Anna May sullenly obeyed. Zack judged that she had started out as a percentage girl at the Good Time and had graduated or been demoted, according to the point of view, to a place at Box Springs Ranch. The Ax had entered the room and was glowering at her, promising her that her attitude toward a stranger like Zack would bring her trouble later on.

"Anna May's man-crazy," Lila said, indifferent to the fact that Anna May was listening. "Don't get any wrong ideas. She's already spoken for around here."

"Thanks for the information," Zack said. "And you?"

Lila stared at him, surprised in spite of herself. Then she laughed. "You *are* a cool one," she said. "That comes under the head of business to be taken up in the future. There are other matters to be discussed first."

Zack waited. He sensed that she was trying to decide whether to go ahead. He was sure she was waiting for some sign from The Ax. The Ax did not speak.

Lila was forced to go it alone. "All right. We know you are aware of what this place really is."

She paused. Zack heard the faint, but plain chatter of a telegraph sounder. Then that ended. It was as though a door had opened and closed somewhere.

Lila shot a glance at The Ax who turned and left the house, striding angrily. Zack guessed the answer. Evidently the railroad's telegraph line had been tapped, and a hidden wire ran to Box Springs Ranch. By that means the outlaws could keep track of train movements and other railroad information. It was a secret that The Ax apparently had not wanted revealed—at least to Zack.

Zack waited for Lila to do the talking. But she was waiting also, an annoyed frown creasing her brow. The wait went on and on. The new coffee eventually was ready. Zack sipped at the steaming contents of a cup. Still Lila did not break the silence. There was growing tension in her manner, however.

Once more Zack was sure he heard the sounder of a telegraph instrument. Only for a moment, as though a door had been opened and closed again.

The Ax returned. He gave Lila a look. Their eyes locked for an instant. Zack saw that in both of them was a burst of wild, fierce excitement. But along with that there was in both of them apprehension—fear. They had the attitudes of at last finding themselves face-to-face with a situation that fascinated them, but which they also dreaded now that the time had come.

"When?" she asked The Ax.

"Tonight," he said. "It'll be around midnight, but I want to pull out as soon as it comes full dark. I want plenty of time. And no mistakes."

"How many men?"

The Ax thought it over. "The fewer the better. Three ought to be enough. I want Ogallala and Matt Pecos."

"And our friend Keech," Lila said.

The Ax frowned. "I don't understand. I figure it'd be better if—"

Lila cut him off abruptly. "You know the ord—the plan, I mean. Follow it unless you want to find yourself in real trouble."

She looked at Zack. "You're going with The Ax and the boys tonight. It's going to be a surprise party on the Rocky. I'm sure you wouldn't want to miss it."

These people had wrecked trains, murdered and tortured. Zack believed they did not trust him—at least not yet. He decided that they might only be putting him to a test. He took it for granted that this was to be another looting expedition, but the limited number who would ride indicated that it was something far out of the ordinary. By going along with their plan he might learn something valuable about their methods. He was sure he had already come upon some information. Neither Lila nor The Ax were the leader of the highbinders. Lila had almost let slip the fact that they had precise orders as to the night's plan. Those orders must have come by telegraph over the tapped wire.

Both of them were waiting for him to speak. "If it means getting square with the Rocky," he said, "you can count me in."

The Ax had to accept that although Zack could see that he was dubious. "I could swing it with jest the Kid an' Pecos," he grumbled.

"Quit complaining," Lila snapped. "And remember, there's to be no shooting."

That lifted some of the burden off Zack's conscience. Looting a freight car might be condoned for the sake of his main purpose, but he knew that anything involving gunplay might force him to take sides and reveal that purpose. Evidently nothing as drastic as train wrecking was planned in view of the small force The Ax was taking with him. Still, his uneasiness deepened, for he could still see the wild emotions that ran in Lila and The Ax. This was something out of the ordinary for them, something the Box Springs outlaws had never before attempted.

Lila added a touch of cool water to the still-torrid cup that Anna May had petulantly placed in front of her. She kept waiting, trying not to look at Zack. But, being a woman she could not keep it up.

"Aren't you going to ask?" she burst out. "What are you made of—stone?"

The Ax spoke quickly. "Don't bother, fella. You'll find out tonight."

"That's good enough for me," Zack said. He pushed his coffee cup aside and arose, stretching. "Mind if I look around a little? I need to get the kinks out of my legs."

"We mind," The Ax snapped. "We don't wander around much in the open here at the Box. Not in daylight at least. Don't worry about the kinks. You'll get them out before long. You'll be most of the night in the saddle."

"I still don't savvy why the law men don't know about this place," Zack commented.

"What law men?"

"Well, there's Wild Bill Hickok for one."

"He's town marshal an' has his hands full in the Wells. Anyway, he's only one man. The sheriff's a long ways off, an' folks have learned not to be too nosy about the Box."

The Ax studied Zack for a space, then added, "A few have showed up around here. Some of 'em never seemed to find their way back to town to collect what money the Rocky was payin' for snoopin'. Them that did get back had sense enough to keep their mouths shut. 'Specially if they was family men. Sometimes things happened to their wives or kids. Accident-like. We've got good friends in the Wells. Lots of 'em. The Rocky ain't too popular there, except among them that work for the railroad. Even some of them railroaders sort of go along with us."

If there had been any exhilaration at the thought of the spice of danger in associating with these criminals, it faded entirely within Zack and was replaced by a sick and burning rage. He had already seen proof that they had committed murder and torture. Evidently there was nothing they would stop at to tighten the reign of terror they patently held over Sioux Wells and its citizens. The twinges of conscience that had been nagging him over infiltrating this organization also died.

He knew that Lila was studying him, trying to read his thoughts. Something of the revulsion he was feeling toward her and all these ruffians must have touched her, for her mouth tightened a little, angrily.

"There's one thing I want to make clear," The Ax said. "If shootin' is needed, I shoot. An' shoot to kill, no matter who it is I shoot at. I think of myself first, no matter what anybody says. I ain't too happy about this thing tonight."

"He's only trying to throw a scare into you, Keech," Lila said quickly. "He doesn't believe you take us seriously enough. This is not a thing that will call for gunplay."

She was only trying to smooth over the situation. There was a bitter, mirthless smile on The Ax's thick lips as he turned and stalked out of the door. "We ride tonight," he spoke before he closed the door.

The fading daylight showed the faces of the two men who were waiting in the barn when The Ax led Zack out of the hideout and into the meeting place among stalls unused by horses for a long time.

Zack peered closer. "Well, well!" he said. "We seem to have met before. The Ogallala Kid is the name, I believe. And this other one calls himself Matt Pecos."

The Ogallala Kid snarled something in a mumble that Zack could not interpret, but did not need to. He was well aware that the Kid had less than no affection for him. Nor did his companion. Matt Pecos said nothing, merely stared with flat eyes. He wore a strip of court plaster on his chin. Zack could not recall having landed a blow there, but evidently he was the person responsible, for the man fingered his injury, and his stare was that of one who was promising that he would never forget his grudge.

"You remember them, I see," The Ax said sardonically.

"Very much so," Zack said. "But we're not what you might call old friends."

"I won't ask you boys to shake hands," The Ax said, "but I want you to know that we're on the same side tonight, and I don't stand for anybody settling personal matters while we're on a job for the organization. Keep that in mind. We pull together or somebody finds hisself where he don't want to be—which might be in a bed six feet under."

Six saddled horses were waiting. They shaped up as sturdy animals, solid of leg and haunch—the sort of mounts men would want under them if called on to out-distance pursuers.

"You take the black gelding," The Ax said to Zack, indicating a powerfully built animal.

Zack adjusted the stirrups to his satisfaction and mounted. The saddle didn't particularly suit him, mainly because it was creakily new—more loot from a Rocky freight car, no doubt.

The other three mounted, and they rode away into the deepening darkness, leading the two spare animals whose stirrups had been tied across the saddles. The Ax set a leisurely pace as they headed away from the ranch, where, true to its pose as a rundown homestead, the only light was from a lamp in the kitchen.

However, Zack again heard the faint clatter of the telegraph sounder. The Ax called a halt and rode away into the darkness alone. He returned after a few minutes, breathing hard.

"It'll be a sweet long time before that fool brass pounder opens that door while that thing is tickin'," he snarled. "I cuffed him around some."

They rode on again in silence. This latest episode concerning the telegraph brought up questions in Zack's mind. On the face of it The Ax apparently had decided there was no point in keeping the presence of the tapped line a secret from him. That meant that he was being accepted at face value. Still, there was an uneasiness deep in his mind whose source he could not determine.

It was the Ogallala Kid who finally spoke. "I don't savvy this, Axel? There's only the four of us, countin' this cowboy. Just what are we supposed to be up to?"

"Shut up!" The Ax snapped.

"Cain't a fella even ask a question?" the Kid mumbled. "Seems like me an' Matt ought to know at least where we're goin'."

The Ax twisted in the saddle and glared at him in the starlight. He lapsed into surly silence.

Zack judged that they had traveled little more than two miles when they crossed what apparently was an abandoned stretch of railroad track. It was weed-grown, the rails appearing rusty in the faint light. Evidently it was a spur off the main line of the Rocky Mountain Express which was no longer used.

They paralleled this, still traveling at a slow pace. Finally, The Ax who had been rising in the saddle and peering ahead, gave a grunt of satisfaction. "Here we are," he said.

Zack made out the vague picket line of telegraph poles and saw the glint of steel rails. They had reached the main line of the railroad.

The Ax flared a match to look at his watch, then headed north, with the railroad track nearby. After less than a mile he seemed satisfied with the lay of the land and pulled up his horse. "All right," he said, dismounting. "We'll hang around here a while. It might be quite a few hours."

"Ain't no freight trains due along here 'til ten o'clock," the Ogallala Kid said uneasily. "An' with only four of us what could we do?"

"Shut up!" The Ax replied. "An' keep shut."

He led the way a short distance from the line of track and into the cover of a small gully. They tied up the horses to stunted brush and settled down to wait. As The Ax had predicted, the wait went on and on.

Eventually they heard the distant rumble of an approaching train. It was coming from the direction of Sioux Wells. The Kid and Matt Pecos, who had found places to recline while they puffed cigarettes, got to their feet expectantly.

But The Ax did not move. "Keep yore fool heads down," he said. "We don't want to be seen."

The train rumbled past and the sound receded into the distance, then died. The wait went on.

The Ax finally moved to his horse, removed a bundle that was tied to the saddle. He dealt out rolls of grain sacks to Zack and the other two. "Don't put these on 'til the time comes, when I give the word," he said. "An' no shootin' unless I say so. 'Specially at the fellers on the engine. They're some of us."

Zack discovered that the grain sacks were masks, for they had eyeholes cut in them. He found a comfortable place to sit, apart from the others, and waited. The night was warm, fragrant with the perfume of grass and sage. The clean, gentle night breeze touched him. An old moon was rising in the sky. A man could₁ be completely at peace with the world on a night like this, with no regrets for the past, no anxieties for the future. But there was no such tranquillity in him, nor in his three companions. They were all on edge, as taut as a stretched wire. And The Ax was the most nervous of all. He could not rest, but kept rolling cigarette after cigarette and peering at his watch in the matchlight.

Time dragged. Zack's watch told him that midnight was near when The Ax drew a long breath and stood listening. Zack made out the pulse beat of a locomotive far away. The sound also came from the direction of Sioux Wells to the north.

"Come on!" The Ax snapped. "Leave them horses here."

They left cover and moved nearer the right-of-way. Soon, Zack made out the beam of the engine's headlight fingering across the flats, appearing, disappearing. Finally, the light was sweeping the stretches of plains nearby, picking out larger clumps of brush, giving golden glow to outcrops of boulders. Then it was bearing down upon them, lighting up the rails and ties.

"Git them masks on," The Ax ordered. Zack pulled the grain sack over his head and adjusted it so that he could peer through the eyeholes. The other three were similarly arrayed.

The Ax had brought from a saddlebag a bull's-eye lantern. He lighted it and Zack saw that it was equipped with a red lens. The locomotive was bearing down on their position now.

"Hell, Axel!" Matt Pecos snarled. "It's only one car. A passenger car, an' all dark an' looks empty. What'n blazes!"

"All you need to do is follow orders," The Ax gritted. "Anybody what makes any mistakes will pay fer it."

He began snapping the shutter of the bull's-eye, sending lances of crimson light down the track. The beat from the stack of the locomotive slowed instantly. Zack heard the grind of brakes on sanded tracks. The Ax shifted to a white lens on the lantern, which gave better light and in its beam Zack could see the face of the engineer, who was leaning from the window of the cab, peering with the attitude of a man who had been expecting something like this. The fireman was standing in the gangway, also taking this calmly enough.

The engine came to a stop. The Ax ran to the steps of the single car back of the tender. Zack saw the gleam of polished brass and gold paint. This was the ornate private palace car that he had seen standing on a sidetrack in the Sioux Wells railroad yards, and which The Ax had said belonged to J. K. Tolliver, owner of the Rocky Mountain Express.

The Ax leaped up the steps to the platform of the palace car, followed by the Ogallala Kid. The door was locked, and he blew off the lock with two blasts from his six-shooter.

A girl screamed in the car. The frightened voice of an older woman also arose, demanding to know what in condemnation was going on. Zack had heard those voices before. They belonged to Granny Julia Smith and her beautiful granddaughter.

He followed The Ax and the Ogallala Kid into the car. The Ax bellowed an order for Matt Pecos to stand guard outside. The beam of the bull's-eye showed that they were in the narrow corridor that contained sleeping compartments, which occupied half of the car. Beyond was a lounge section with brocaded chairs and settees, and a small kitchen at the rear. Rich quarters.

"Git dressed an' come out, you two!" The Ax bellowed. "Right quick. Pronto! Quit yowlin' in there, young lady! An' you can stop cussin', old lady. You won't git hurt."

"Go to blazes!" the grandmother screeched. "What kind of scoundrels air you, tryin' to terrorize two poor, defenseless ladies in the middle of the night? What do you want? If it's money you're after, you're wastin' your time. We ain't got more'n a few dollars between us."

"Come out, afore I have to come in an' drag you out!" The Ax snarled. "You ain't goin' to be hurt. But you're goin' with us whether you want to or not."

"Goin' with you? Where?"

"You'll find out. We know who you are."

"Who are they?" Zack asked.

"The old biddy's real name is Julia K. Tolliver. I don't know what the K stands for. Cussedness, maybe. The young one's name is Anita Tolliver."

"Well, I'll be damned!" Zack said. "I should have known."

"Them two own this here Rocky Mountain Express, lock, stock an' barrel, between them," The Ax said. "They go under the name of Smith around Sioux Wells, for they don't want men to know they're workin' for a railroad owned by petticoats."

Chapter 8

The Ax pounded on the doors of two of the compartments with his guns. "Come out right now!" he roared.

"I'll come out when I'm dressed proper, an' not before, you blasted rascal!" the elder woman replied. "The first one that tries to come through that door before I say so gits a slug in his belly, an' that goes for my granddaughter's room too. I got a gun here that will do the talkin' for me."

"All right, all right!" The Ax said hastily. "But don't try any shenanigans. Before you come out, push that gun out ahead of you on the floor. Don't try anything foolish, like goin' out a window. We've got men on watch outside. You'd only git caught, an' maybe git hurt in the bargain."

Anita Tolliver was the first to emerge. She was still trying to twist her hair into a semblance of order, and was jabbing at hairpins with nervous fingers. She had hurriedly pulled on a skirt, blouse and shoes. She gave a startled little cry of fear when she saw the grotesque shapes of the three men in the masks, but recovered, refusing to show panic.

"What are you going to do with us?" she demanded.

"You'll jest be our guests fer a little while," The Ax said.

"Watch out fer that filly," the Ogallala Kid warned. "I happen to know she packs a derringer."

"Well, well!" Anita Tolliver said. "It's nice to know at least one of you. You're the coward who shoots game

104

from railroad cars, then leaves them wounded to die."

"You fool!" The Ax snarled at the Kid. "Won't you ever learn to keep your yap shut?"

Julia Tolliver opened the door of her quarters and pushed a six-shooter ahead of her into the passageway with the toe of her slipper. The Ax snatched up the weapon.

"Now for thet derringer, you," he said, addressing Anita Tolliver. "Hand it over."

The girl hesitated, then shrugged and turned away. Evidently she was carrying the small weapon in her garter. When she turned again, she had the derringer in her hand. Reluctantly, she surrendered it to the outlaw.

"Don't you know that they string you up without a trial for mistreatin' women?" Julia Tolliver said scornfully. She was fully dressed, evidently even to stays beneath her neat, dark dress. She had donned a small bonnet and had a knitted shawl around her shoulders.

"Keep quiet!" The Ax snarled. "I'll do all the talkin'."

"Don't you ever again try to shut me up," Julia Tolliver rasped. "I'll see you do a jig at the end of a rope for this night's work."

"Hold your tongue, you old harridan!" The Ax raged. "I'd put a slug in you if it wasn't that—"

He decided not to finish it. "If it wasn't for what?" Anita Tolliver demanded. "Just what are you going to do with us?"

"Never mind that," he said. "Now git back in this sleepin' room, an' stay there. Don't close the door. You'll be watched every minute."

The Tollivers hesitated. Zack could see that they were mortally afraid, but trying desperately to show a brave front.

"Move!" The Ax said. There was a deadliness in him, a viciousness that belied his promises that they would not be hurt. Anita hurriedly seized her grandmother's arm and drew her inside one of the compartments. Zack watched them seat themselves close together on the berth and hold hands.

"You stay here," The Ax said, stabbing a finger at the Ogallala Kid. "Jest see thet the ladies stay there too. An' don't try to git gay with them."

"You," he said to Zack. "Come with me."

Zack followed him to the platform. Matt Pecos was standing on guard alongside the track. "You fetch the horses, Pecos," The Ax said. "See to it thet none git away. We're goin' to need 'em."

"Whar to?" Pecos asked.

"To that spot on the old Crown Point sidin' where we have worked before," The Ax said. "We're takin' this car up there an' spot it out of sight."

Then The Ax yelled ahead to the engineer. "All right, Hank. Git goin'!"

"You mean on up the line?" the engineer yelled back.

"Blast it!" The Ax screeched. "Can't anybody learn to do what they're told without askin' a lot of fool questions."

"But—!"

The Ax, cursing, scrambled up the short iron ladder to the water tank deck of the tender. He had his gun in hand, and was glaring down into the locomotive cab. "Git rollin'," he raged. "Afore I put a slug in you."

The engineer obeyed with such haste that the steam boxes gushed like geysers, the stack exploded into bellowing life and the drive wheels spun. Zack was staggered against the car's door, but managed to hang on until he recovered his balance.

The wheels found traction and the equipment got under way. The Ax had vanished, having scrambled down into the cab of the engine. Zack moved to the platform, swinging out by the handrails and looking ahead. He saw the fireman on the running board alongside the boiler.

Then the headlight died, and the engine was moving along unlighted rails.

Presently the pace eased as power slackened. Zack could see the head and shoulders of The Ax jutting from the gangway of the engine. The man was peering ahead, evidently seeking some landmark.

Then the brakes were applied and the train slowed, then stopped. The Ax leaped to the ground and ran ahead. Zack heard the squeaking of metal, and The Ax shouted, "All right! Come ahead!"

The train crept ahead again and swerved off the main line onto a spur track. No doubt it was the weedy, overgrown track they had crossed some distance west earlier in the evening, the Crown Point siding.

The engineer halted the equipment again, and metallic sounds told that The Ax had rethrown the switch. The man came running out of the darkness and mounted the steps to the lounge car platform where Zack waited.

"All right, Hank!" he shouted. "Pull ahead again. I'll tell you when to stop."

"Dang it, Axel!" the engineer shouted back. "This here spur gits more risky every time I run over it. We'll likely wind up ridin' on the ties."

"Take it slow," The Ax answered. "If it looks too risky, stop 'til we kin make sure. I don't want this outfit to be hung up out here in the open come daybreak."

The train got under way again, very slowly as the engineer felt his way along.

"What'n blazes is this all about?" the Ogallala Kid asked.

"What do you keer?"

"I got a right to ask," the Kid said sullenly.

"What right?"

"It's like the old lady said. They don't take kindly to roughin' up women in these parts. I've heerd of some terrible things that has happened to some what did things like that."

"You kin git off right now if you want. Either that or quit whinin'." The Ax had his six-shooter in his hand, and it was apparent he was ready to use it.

The Kid subsided. He had been very close to death and knew it. "Keep yore shirt on, Axel," he croaked. "I didn't mean nothin'. I just don't know what this is all about."

The Ax laughed with contempt. He shoved past Zack, walked down the corridor into the lounge section of the car. He moved to a window and kept peering out. After a time he hurried back to the platform and leaned from the steps. "We're about there, Hank. Stop in that cut ahead as soon as you're sure we're between banks high enough to hide this outfit."

The train crept along for a short distance. Zack could see brush-grown banks rising higher on either side of the track. Then the equipment jolted to a stop. The Ax leaped to the ground and surveyed the situation. "All right," he shouted. "This is good enough."

He returned to the car, walked to the open door of the compartment where the Tollivers waited. "Come out!" he commanded.

Anita Tolliver and her grandmother slowly emerged. "What do we do now?" she said.

"Wait a while. There'll be horses brought up directly. Kin the old lady ride?"

Julia Tolliver bristled. "I was ridin' high-steppin' horses afore you was born, you rascal. Where you takin' us?"

"Out to view the scenery," The Ax said.

Julia turned, peering through the window of the compartment. "I'd say we're on the old Crown Point spur that we built back into the hills to bring out gravel an' timber when we was constructin' the Rocky through this country."

"Could be," The Ax replied.

The wait did not last long. Zack heard the sound of hoofs and knew that Matt Pecos was bringing up the horses.

"All right, ladies," The Ax said. "We're all gittin' off here."

Zack was first to alight. He waited to help Anita Tolliver from the step of the car, but she knocked his hand aside, and turned to assist her grandmother to the ground. "Don't touch me, you scum!" she said.

The Ax, pistol in hand, followed, accompanied by the Kid. "Stay here, you two," The Ax called to the engineer and fireman. "I'll have horses brung over to take you to the ranch. You won't be needed fer a little while. Lila will tell you what to do."

"What the hell, Axel!" the engineer protested. "This special will be missed, an' it'll be found sooner or later. What's Joe an' me goin' to say about what happened to us?"

"That'll all be taken care of," The Ax said. "Now do what I say."

He turned and gave young Anita Tolliver a shove. "March!" he snarled.

"What about our luggage?" she demanded.

"Never mind that," The Ax said. "If'n it's clothes you need I kin skeer up enough to fix you two up and a hundred like you."

"Stolen from the railroad, of course," Julia Tolliver said wrathfully.

"March, I say!" The Ax rasped, and they all went stumbling over crooked ties and through weeds out of the cut to where Matt Pecos and the horses were waiting. The two women were lifted aboard the spare mounts and left to manage as best they could with their skirts.

"If you was halfway human, you'd have brung side-saddles so we could ride as ladies should," Julia Tolliver complained. "How did you know we was on that car?"

"We know everything."

"Where are you taking us?"

"Shut up!" The Ax snarled, resorting to his particular way of ending discussions.

"I told you not to say things like that to me ag'in!" Julia Tolliver snapped. She swung the ends of the long reins and caught The Ax across the cheek with whip-like force that brought a yelp of pain and fury from him. He yanked his horse close, a fist clenched, and would have smashed the elderly woman in the face.

Zack also kicked his horse within reach and managed to grasp The Ax's arm and halt the blow. This destroyed The Ax's balance and he nearly fell from his horse.

He recovered, dragging himself back into the saddle and whirled on Zack, his pistol in his hand. Again he was in a killing rage. It faded, for he was looking into the bore of Zack's gun inches from his face.

"I don't like any part of this," Zack said. "I didn't declare myself into this game to haze women around. And I don't stand for a man mauling a woman—and an old lady at that."

"She's got it comin'," The Ax gritted. But he now had control of himself and holstered the pistol. However, Zack doubted that he was responsible for quelling the storm. The Ax had thought of other and better reasons for not pursuing the matter. "But the next time you git out of hand—" he growled at Julia Tolliver. He let it ride there, but it was mere bluster now.

"You might as well take off that feed bag you've got over your ugly head," she said. "I know you. Your name is Jim Axel, and you was a straw boss on one of our track-layin' gangs when we was buildin' the Rocky. My son fired you for petty stealin', booted you out of camp. An' now you're still stealin' from us Tollivers."

The Ax yanked off his mask and hurled it away. His two outlaws followed that example, glad to be free of the confining burlap. Zack also rid himself of the disguise. The thought had struck him that the Tollivers might show some sign of gladness when they saw they had an ally at hand, but he felt that they had recognized his voice, also, by this time. They were equal to the occasion. They only glared scornfully at him in the yellow moonlight.

"Well, well," Anita Tolliver said. "This *is* a surprise. So you've joined the highbinders. I suppose that figures. I knew you had a grudge against the Rocky, but I really didn't think you would stoop so low as to kidnap women."

"Be quiet," Zack said. He was playing out his role, but in him was a chill realization. There could be only one answer to the removal of the masks. It was never intended that Julia Tolliver and her granddaughter would live to identify their captors.

The Tollivers must have understood this also, for Julia Tolliver had to try repeatedly before she could overcome the quaver in her voice and make herself heard. "Just what do you expect to get out of all this?"

"I've said all I'm goin' to say," The Ax growled. "No more talk, lest I have you gagged."

They were heading in the general direction of Box Springs Ranch, but Zack, after a time, discovered that their route was more westerly and would carry them a distance wide of that hideout. They rode in silence, the women boxed in by the outlaws to prevent any attempt at a break to escape.

Presently they entered broken country, with the horses laboring up rocky ascents, following the tumbling course of a fast stream. Jagged buttes and rims arose around them. Julia Tolliver was obviously having a trying time of it in the bulky saddle, and Anita was staying close at her side as much as possible, attempting to assist her.

"Dang it, 'Nita," Julia complained. "Quit cluckin' over me like I was stove up an' crippled. This cussed saddle is too big fer me, an' I rattle around in it like a dried pea in a pod, but I've rid worse, an' I ain't made of sugar an' salt. I won't melt."

Dawn was lighting the sky. Through breaks in the patchwork of ridges and low hills Zack sighted Box Springs Ranch only two miles or so away on the flats below the cover of the hills that they were following.

They were now following a faint horse trail, evidently seldom used, although there were the marks of a few fresh hoof prints. Riders had traveled this route both ways lately.

They emerged into a small flat where a spring was the source of a small stream that wound across the flat to join the bigger creek. Grass, aspen, spruce and pine grew here. There was a small corral, empty now and a log gear shed that also seemed to be seldom used. Dominating the layout was a well-built log cabin with a high gable, shake roof and a small veranda of rustic wood. The faded pelt of a grizzly was nailed to one wall along with wolf and cougar skins. The antlers of elk, deer and bighorns decorated the main house and gear shed.

A hunting lodge by the looks, Zack surmised. There was no sign of life about the house. The Ax led the way past without comment. They rounded an outthrust shoulder of a higher ledge and came upon a rude, sagging log shack which crouched, animal-like against the base of a cliff.

"All right," The Ax said. "We're here. Light down."

Zack slid from his horse and moved to help Julia Tolliver. Continuing the role they were playing, she slapped his hands away. "I don't want to be touched by the likes of you," she snapped, and accepted assistance from her granddaughter.

The Ax was standing a pace back. Before Zack realized what was happening his six-shooter had been snatched from its holster. He whirled and found himself facing his own gun, cocked and in the hands of The Ax.

"Put up yore arms, cowboy," The Ax said harshly. "It'd be a pleasure to put a bullet in you. We don't like spies. We don't like 'em none at all."

"What are you talking about?" Zack demanded.

"We know all about you, mister. You tried to worm your way into our bunch because Julia Tolliver promised to pay your claim for them stampeded cattle if you sent all of us to the gallows and the pen."

"But it was you people who invited me in," Zack protested.

"Sure, sure. You've heard of the spider and the fly, haven't you. Didn't it ever occur to you that we were making it easy for you to get this far? Too easy. You took us for fools. The fact is we sort of needed you. We took you along on this thing tonight because we figured these two gals would give us less trouble if they thought they had their hired spy along to maybe help them when the sign was right. And we had other reasons."

"What other reasons?"

"You better hope that you never find out," The Ax replied. "Matt, git the leg irons. You'll find 'em lyin' in the shack just inside the door. I put them there myself when I rode over here yesterday. I'll keep the key. No point in tyin' up his arms. He ain't goin anywhere when he's hobbled. Make sure he ain't got any hideouts, such as a knife or palm gun."

Zack and the two women were led at gunpoint to the shack and pushed through its crooked door. The clank of iron sounded and Matt Pecos brought up the leg irons.

"Courtesy of the Rocky Mountain Express," the man

said, grinning, as he clamped the irons around Zack's ankles. "These things was bein' shipped to the law dogs in the gold camps, but it happened that we inherited them an' figured we might have use for 'em from time to time. We was right."

The chain connecting the shackles was little more than a foot long, limiting Zack's activity to awkward hobbling. Remembering Jimmy Broom, he was wondering why they were permitting him to stay alive at all. The Ax guessed what was in his mind and answered the question. "You ain't worth near as much on the hoof as the hen an' chick," he said. "But you're worth enough to pay us for our trouble, if need be."

"How's that?" Zack asked.

"You're Brandy Ben Keech's son, ain't you? That's another reason we scooped you up in our net. He's on his way to the Indian agency up north to sell ninety thousand dollars' worth of beef, ain't he, barrin' a few hundred head that you say were lost in the stampede. Ninety thousand ain't in it with somethin' else we got in mind, but it ain't pocket change either. We got two barrels to our gun. If one don't bring down the big game, maybe the other will. An' maybe both barrels will score."

Zack looked at the Tollivers and saw the waxen set of their faces. More and more they were realizing that there was little hope they would live through this.

"Brandy Ben has a reputation for being a dangerous man to try to bluff," Zack said.

"It happens we ain't bluffin'."

"He won't pay. I know him."

"He'll change his mind after we start sendin' him little souvenirs. Such as an ear or two. If that don't convince him, we'll start on yore fingers an' toes. Or a nose. What kind of a father would turn his back on things like that, just to save a few dollars?"

"And then you'd have him hounding you the rest of

your lives," Zack said. "I know him. And there are a few more Keech's down in Texas who would join in the hunt."

The Ax tried to snort scornfully, but it was a failure. Evidently he had never given a thought to being marked for vengeance, and it worried him. He changed the subject and turned to the Tollivers.

"As for you two, I warn you not to try to git away. There'll be men on watch outside every minute. You couldn't git far even if you managed to sneak away. We've got dogs to bring up that'd run you down in no time."

He and his companions left the shack. They closed the door which was built of slabs, and Zack heard them bracing it securely with more slabs. Zack hopped to the door which was so poorly fitted there were slits that gave views of the surroundings. The Ax and Matt Pecos were heading on foot around the arm of the ledge, evidently in the direction of the hunting lodge. The Ogallala Kid was making himself comfortable on a log which he had dragged against a tree. He seated himself there, a rifle and his six-shooters handy, his position commanding their place of confinement.

Zack looked around the interior. "There's no place like home," he said.

The shack was about ten by twelve feet, with a dirt floor. The one window was fitted with a four-pane sash, but the outside was covered with crisscrossed barbed wire. There were two mattresses in the corners, along with sheets, blankets and pillows. One of the pallets had been used. The thought struck Zack that this was where Jimmy Broom might have been held until he was tortured for information and murdered.

He discovered a small opening at the rear. Hopping to it he discovered that the shack had been built as an addition to a dugout under the base of the cliff. The dugout probably had been the quarters of the original resident, a hunter and trapper, no doubt, and the shack had been added later.

"A real two-room palace," he said. "I'll take the rear bedroom. You ladies can sleep in the parlor."

"Sleep!" Julia Tolliver sniffed. "Who'll be able to sleep with these cutthroats waitin' to murder us?"

"What's this all about?" Zack asked.

"I wish I knew," Julia Tolliver said dolefully. "I never been kidnapped before. If it's money they want, they're wastin' their time. Me'n 'Nita are as poor as church mice. We've sold about everythin', tryin' to keep the Rocky goin'. Fact is, we was headin' east to try to sweet-talk bankers into loanin' us money, an' to sell the palace car."

"To sell it?"

"One of the bigwigs on the Union Pacific had offered me five thousand dollars for it, an' we was takin' it east to close the deal. Me an' 'Nita couldn't afford any longer to ride in a private car. We ride the cushions like everybody else, as you saw the day you got mixed up with us when that skunk shot the antelope. In addition we was runnin' scared last night."

"Scared. Why were you two alone in that fancy car?"

"Bill Hickok come to us yesterday an' advised us to git out of the Wells, an' git out fast. Somebody had tipped him off that something big was in the wind an' that us Tollivers was mixed up in it."

"Who tipped him off?"

"He didn't say, except that the person was a friend of both him and us, and that there wasn't any question but that the information was reliable. We hired Bill to come in an' try to break up this gang that's robbin' us blind, but it's been too tough a job even for him. He's bein' watched every minute, an' that attempt to kill him the other night wasn't the first, an' likely won't be the last. We got hit by our biggest loss just recently. Forty thousand dollars in gold dust that was brought by wagon from the mines to our end of steel at Summit, which is forty miles west of the Wells. The train was stuck up after if had gone through the Wells, bound east. We got to make that up to the shippers."

"How? You just said you were broke."

She made a helpless gesture. "How would I know? Another thing I don't know is how these rascals knew me an' 'Nita was aboard the car last night. We sneaked into it after dark as it set in the yards. Even the two on the engine wasn't told. They only thought they'd been called to take that empty palace car on a special run down to Buffalo Junction. Only Hickok an' Frank Niles knew we was aboard."

"Niles?"

It was Anita who spoke. "Frank was the only one with authority to call in the crew and order an engine out of the shop," she said slowly.

Nobody said anything for a space. It was Zack who broke the silence. "Did you know that the railroad telegraph line is tapped? There's a line running to their headquarters at a place called Box Springs Ranch, which isn't more than a couple of miles from here. That's how they've been keeping tab on which shipments are worth hitting. I think they've been using that old railroad spur at times for unloading freight cars. I think the word came through to Box Springs yesterday afternoon to The Ax that you two were to be on that special run last night."

"Word? From who?"

"Box Springs is a big setup," Zack said. "On the face of it you'd think it was a homestead on its last legs, but there are underground storehouses and haystacks that aren't haystacks but caches for what they steal. That young woman who calls herself Lila and runs the Good Time in Sioux Wells, is in on it. She seems to give the orders. Maybe she's the brains back of all this."

"I doubt if that hussie has got a real brain in her head," Anita spoke scornfully. "I suppose men like you are dazzled by good looks and a shape."

"She does have points there," Zack said.

Anita uttered only another disparaging sniff. Her grandmother spoke hastily. "Never mind discussin' things like that. I know the gal. Her real name is Martha Kelly, an' I ain't surprised to hear she's mixed up with the highbinders. Now why didn't some of them detectives we hired find out about this Box Springs hangout?"

"Some probably did," Zack said, "but didn't live to tell about it, like Jimmy Broom, or were too scared to talk. How long has all this highbinding been going on?"

"It started more'n two years ago," Julia sighed. "It was only petty theft at first, but it kept snowballin'. That's why I finally hollered for help from Bill Hickok. I met Bill years ago when my husband was layin' track for the Union Pacific an' I was helpin' with the books. Bill was scoutin' for the Army at the time."

"Your husband is dead, I take it?"

"Yes, God rest his soul. He was killed when a work train went through a temporary bridge not long after he had started buildin' the Rocky. Our son, who was 'Nita's father, took over an' finished the Rocky beyond Sioux Wells. We had put every cent we had in the world into the Rocky. When these highbinders hit us we had to stop construction short of the mountains. We'd really do business if we could git to the gold camps. Even so, it was a payin' proposition until the thieves got busy. Me an' 'Nita own it all. She lost her maw an' paw two years ago. Indians hit a stagecoach on which they were ridin' outside Denver City."

"Who besides Hickok and Frank Niles know that you two are J. K. Tolliver between you and not the Smiths?" Zack asked.

"Must be quite a few in Sioux Wells," Julia admitted.

"The Wells wasn't more'n a grease spot at first, but there's a few around who was with us when we built into it, an' set up a station an' a water tank. There's Jud Gregg at the hotel. He's known us for years. An' Sid Crain, the justice of peace. Ed Hake used to hunt buffalo fer us. There's quite a few others around who know who we really are, some of whom I don't care to name at this time. They're old friends. It might be what you call an open secret in the Wells. Our only reason is that railroad men are a proud lot. They don't like to be told that they're bein' bossed by womenfolk."

Zack eyed Anita. "Just why did you come down on me those times after I had trouble with that big hulk of an engineer who stampeded our herd."

"I'm railroad," she said. "I was given a railroad spike to play with in my crib. You're not railroad. To me you were just a big, overbearing cowboy not fit to humiliate people like us by knocking out our best man with one punch. I wanted you to lose. I wanted Stan Durkin to wallop you all over the street. But you disappointed me. Twice."

"I'll be careful to avoid you if I lock horns with Durkin again," he said. "But he's a sucker for a right cross. You did more damage to me than Durkin."

Chapter 9

Zack moved along the walls of the shack in the hope he might find something that would offer a chance of bursting free. He crawled into the dugout and inspected it almost inch by inch. It was all wasted effort.

The Tollivers helped as best they could, all maintaining silence so as to not arouse the Ogallala Kid's inspection. They all finally gave it up. The Tollivers sat together on one of the pallets. Zack used a wall of the shack for support and sat legs outstretched.

The morning advanced. They heard sounds, the sound of voices. But it was only the Ogallala Kid changing over the guard duty to Matt Pecos.

They continued to wait, a listless apathy claiming them. They aroused at every faint sound, but always they sank back, discovering that it was the scamper of a bird over their roof, or the changing of the guard. Even The Ax stood a three-hour vigil.

The torpid heat of afternoon began to invade their quarters. Still nothing. Zack became aware of nagging thirst. He began thinking of water, of cooling springs at which he had partaken in the past, of creeks and rivers in which he had swum. He tried to shake away such phantoms. They kept rising in his mind. He finally lifted his voice in sudden fury. "How about some food and water?"

He knew that The Ax was on guard. But there was no reply. He got to his feet, hopped to the door and pounded on the heavy slabs, shaking the barrier. "You heard me, Axel!" he shouted. "What are you trying to do —torture women? At least bring them water."

Still no answer. Julia Tolliver spoke wanly, "Looks like they don't care whether we suffer or not."

"What are they up to?" he asked.

"Maybe it'd be just as well if we never found out," she said grimly. "But I'm gettin' somethin' of an idea."

"What kind of an idea?"

"I could be wrong. No use borrowin' more trouble than we're already in. I reckon we'll find out sooner or later what this is all about if we wait long enough."

They waited. The afternoon stretched out interminably. Julia Tolliver stretched out on a pallet, attempting to sleep, but it was a failure. Anita moved about their crowded quarters, driven by growing tension. She paused often at Zack's side, but always found that she had nothing to say. He spent the time working at the shackles. It was futile effort, but at least it kept his mind out of other avenues—dark avenues.

Twilight came. And still no sign that their captors had any intention of heeding the demands Zack kept repeating that they be given water and food. It was apparent to Zack now that the real purpose was to weaken their spirit so that they would be more amenable to whatever plan was in store for them.

Full darkness had fallen when they heard the approach of a rider. Zack pulled himself to his feet, and he and the Tollivers crowded to slits in the door peering. But their limited view of the surroundings told them nothing. Apparently the arrival had dismounted at the hunting lodge. After that they heard momentary rumor of voices. Then a door closed, and silence came.

The wait finally ended. The Ax came striding to the shack. The bars were lifted and the door opened. They were blinded by the beam of the bull's-eye lantern in The

Ax's hand. Zack made out the dim shapes of the Kid and Matt Pecos at the shoulder of The Ax.

"Come out you two women!" The Ax said harshly. He came into the shack, seized Anita Tolliver by the arm, sending her staggering toward the door where the Kid grasped her and hustled her outside. The Ax pushed Julia ahead of him and out of the door.

Zack hopped toward the man, a fist clenched, but The Ax was carrying a wagon-spoke club, dangling by a strap from his wrist, and used it. The club landed a glancing blow on Zack's head and sent him reeling, stunned against a wall.

Then they were gone and the door was tightly barred shut again.

"You devils!" he heard Anita Tolliver scream. Then they were gone out of hearing.

Silence again settled over the camp. Time passed, time whose length he could not judge. He had recovered from the glancing blow. It had brought another streak of blood which had dried. He stood at the door, peering, listening. And still no sound that would tell him anything.

Presently they came again, The Ax with his club and bull's-eye lantern, the other two thugs with their guns. The door was opened.

"Tie his arms," The Ax ordered. "An' make blasted sure they *are* tied."

Zack was seized by the desperadoes and his arms were lashed to his sides.

"Start movin'!" The Ax said, and poked the muzzle of a six-shooter into his back.

He was pushed out of the shack and half-dragged along by the Kid and Matt Pecos. They rounded the rock ledge and The Ax called a halt when they reached the shake-roofed hunting lodge. "All right, you two," he said to his companions. "There's a jug over by the water trough. Help yourselves—but don't git drunk. We've all got some more work to do tonight. I'll call you when you're needed. An', above all, don't git curious. Stay away from the house."

The two evidently knew better than to ask questions, for they walked hurriedly away. The Ax opened a door and pushed Zack ahead of him into the house.

It was a big room. Game pelts and woven rugs adorned the walls and floor. A long table of handsawed design, with a polished cedar top dominated the room. Easy chairs and two davenports, made in the rustic style, stood along the walls. Antler racks held a liberal display of hunting rifles and fowling pieces.

A single oil lamp stood on the table, bearing a shade which restricted its glow. Julia and Anita Tolliver sat at the near end of the table, side by side, their backs turned to Zack and The Ax. Their hands, unbound, lay on the table. They seemed to be caught in some sort of a trance. He realized it was cold fear that gripped them.

Another figure sat at the far end of the table. It was a grotesque, formless shape. Zack realized that what he was looking at in the shaded light was a man wearing one of the shapeless grain-sack masks. Two cocked six-shooters lay on the table at his side. An inkstand stood nearby, and smoke from an expensive, lighted cigar coiled up from an ash tray where it had been placed.

The Ax pushed Zack closer to the table. The masked man spoke. "You know what to do, Axel, if he gets rough."

Then the man addressed the Tollivers. "I had hoped you would be reasonable and not force me to take drastic measures to convince you that I'm offering you the best way out. Anything that happens from now on will be on your conscience, Mrs. Tolliver."

Zack recognized that voice. So had the Tollivers. "You treacherous devil!" Anita Tolliver said huskily. "I had begun to suspect, several days ago, that something was wrong with you, but wouldn't let myself actually believe it. To think that we were fools to treat you as a friend, to trust you even up to a few days ago."

Julia Tolliver spoke bitterly. "You might as well take off that mask, Frank. You was the only one besides Hickok who knew we were aboard that car last night. Take it off. We all know who you are."

The masked man laughed. He was Frank Niles, division head of the Rocky. "I prefer to keep it on," he said. "I never doubted but that you people would recognize my voice. It really doesn't make any difference. However, except for Axel here, nobody else around here really knows that I am what I might modestly refer to as head of the highbinders. They think that The Ax, or perhaps Lila, might be the one. I prefer that the lesser members continue to remain in doubt."

"You—you thief!" Julia said grimly. "And to think that your brother is in on this too. How could we misjudge men so far?"

"I'm beginning to lose patience with you two," Niles said. "All I'm asking is that you sign this paper. It will only take a moment.

He was tapping a paper that lay on the table beneath his hands. He moved it closer so that even Zack could read the words written in legal penmanship. But they seemed meaningless in the brief glimpse he had.

"Never!" Julia gritted. "Never!"

"What is it?" Zack asked. "What is he asking you to sign?"

"It's an authorization to his brother to sell all our stock in the Rocky."

"Absolutely correct," Niles said. "It is duly witnessed and notarized, as you will note."

"It's hard to believe that both of you could turn out so vile," Anita said. "You two have wormed your way into our confidence while driving us almost into bankruptcy with your gang of thieves. And now you aim to steal the Rocky itself. You probably expect to pick up the stock at a penny on the dollar—and pay for it with the profits from what you stole from us."

"Go to the head of the class," Niles said. His voice was growing ugly. "Once we are in control we will soon get rid of the highbinders. We know who they are, you see, but they don't know who we are, excepting, of course, Jim here and Lila. They are partners with us. The Rocky can be turned again into a prosperous railroad. We expect to be worth a million or more in a year, and more millions when we build on into the camps."

"Like perdition you will," Julia Tolliver said, shaking with anger. "I'll see you in the flames, with the devil pokin' his pitchfork into you before I sign that paper."

"I'm sure you'll change your mind presently," Niles said. "You can't expect Willis and myself to resist such a bargain after we've planned and worked for so long, now could you?"

"Who's Willis?" Zack asked.

Anita answered. "Willis Niles is Frank's older brother. He has been company attorney ever since the Rocky was organized. He holds the title of executive manager, and is chairman of the board. After the death of my father it seemed better to appear that the Rocky was still run by men."

"Can they get away with this kind of fraud?"

It was Niles who answered. "You just heard Anita say that Willis is chairman of the board, company attorney and general manager. Who would question the sale of stock by such an executive in a company on the verge of bankruptcy?"

He dipped the pen into the ink well, arose and moved the document within Julia Tolliver's reach. "Being the senior stockholder it would be proper for you to sign first, my dear," he said.

Instead of accepting the pen, Julia Tolliver knocked it from his hand. Niles stood for an instant, his eyes cold with rage, and malevolent. Zack believed the man was about to use his fists on the frail, elderly woman, and started to move forward to once again attempt to intervene, but The Ax gripped his arm, holding him back.

Niles thought better of his intention. He forced a smile, bent and retrieved the pen from the floor. "That was foolish of you, Julia," he said. "Don't be difficult again. You're forcing me to take measures that I dislike. Sign."

"No!" Julia said huskily. "Never!"

"It happens I can't spare any more time in debate," Niles said. He spoke to The Ax. "Tear off Keech's shirt. The ladies seem to need an object lesson as to what will happen to them if they continue to be obstinate."

The Ax ripped Zack's shirt from his shoulders, letting the shreds fall from his bound arms. Niles lifted the cigar from the ash tray, blew off the long ash that had formed, blew on the tip until it burned hot and crimson. He moved toward Zack.

"No!" Anita Tolliver choked. "He had no part in this. Why him?"

She tried to arise from the chair. It was then that Zack discovered she and the older woman were tied to the chairs. Niles pushed her roughly back.

"This is one of the reasons we brought this cowboy into our outfit," he said. "We figured you might need a little persuasion."

He advanced on Zack. His features relentless, he slapped Zack with his left hand. A blow that staggered Zack. Then, with deliberation, he pushed the glowing end of the cigar against Zack's bare chest. In spite of himself, Zack uttered a gasp of agony. He felt The Ax's six-shooter hard against his side.

The ugly, acrid tang of burned flesh arose. The act

had been done so casually, so callously he could hardly believe that this was real.

Niles studied the horrified expressions on the faces of Anita Tolliver and her grandmother. They too seemed caught in a dream—a dream of horror. Julia Tolliver's lips were moving, but no sound came out. She was trying to scream, but failing.

Anita was looking at Zack, her dark eyes no longer snapfinger bright, but deep and sunken with pity and misery for him. "I'm so—so sorry," she said brokenly.

Niles drew back a fist with deliberation and smashed Zack in the face. Zack managed to turn his head so that he caught the blow on the cheekbone. He felt blood flow as flesh was gashed. Another blow brought more blood.

Julia Tolliver managed a despairing sound. "Dear God, strike him down!"

"Sign!" Niles gritted.

"Tell him to go to hell," Zack said between lips that were crushed and bleeding.

"Ever see a man's eyeballs burned out?" Niles asked. He held the cigar aloft and once more blew the burning end into a glow. He moved again upon Zack. His face still bore that implacable determination that was driving him. Frank Niles meant exactly what he said. He meant to destroy Zack's sight while the Tollivers watched.

"No! No!" Anita choked. "Don't! Please!"

"Then sign," Niles said icily.

"Don't do it," Zack said hoarsely. "Don't you understand what this means? This man can't afford to let any of us li—"

The glowing cigar came closer. Zack managed to duck, and the crimson end only blistered his cheek. But it had been meant for his eye.

"We'll sign," Julia Tolliver moaned. "We'll sign. Don't torture him any more. We'll sign."

Niles relaxed. "That's better," he said. Again he

casually drew back a fist and smashed it into Zack's face. "You're lucky, Keech," he said. "Or I might have a lot of fun with you. But I've got to get back to the Wells."

He moved back to the table, pushed the document in front of Julia and handed her the pen. She had to try several times before she could control the quivering of her hand enough to affix her name.

Anita Tolliver hesitated. She looked at Zack, her eyes glistening. "Don't sign it," he said.

"And watch this man burn out your eyes?" she sobbed. "You know I can't do that."

She took the pen that Niles handed her and added her name to the paper.

Niles studied the document. "Write in the date," he said to Anita. "This is August 15."

"That was three days ago," she said.

"Do as I say," he replied. "Or would you like to watch Keech really lose an eye?"

She sighed, picked up the pen again and wrote in the date. Niles picked up the document, studied it for a time, then drew on his cigar and blew smoke with an air of complete satisfaction.

He nodded to The Ax. "All right. Take them away."

Then he disappeared through a rear door into an unlighted room that evidently was a kitchen. Another door opened and closed. Zack heard the creak of saddle leather as Niles mounted. Then came the receding sound of hoofs.

The Ax, his pistol covering them, moved to the front door and called out. Matt Pecos and the Ogallala Kid responded, and entered the house. They stared at the blood and signs of torture on Zack and darted uneasy glances at each other, their Adam's apples bobbing.

"This feller," The Ax said, "fell ag'in the lamp an got burned an' bruised some. It was an accident. Right?"

The Kid and his partner swallowed hard. "O' course, o' course!" the Kid said hastily. He had the bravo to sniff the air. "Somebody's been here, smokin' a good cigar, Axel. You don't smoke cigars, now do you?"

"You just keep on askin' smart questions," The Ax said, "until you find yourself in a lot worse shape from fallin' into lamps than this feller here."

"Sure, sure," the Kid agreed quickly. "Where we goin' now?"

"Just fer a little ride," The Ax said. "Saddle up the horses for the three of us, an' fer the ladies an' the cowboy here. Move! Or are you deef? Git them horses up here in a hell of a hurry!"

The pair went stampeding out of the house to where the horses evidently had been corraled. Zack and the Tollivers waited in silence. Zack's injuries bled for a time, then clogged. The burns on his chest continued to plague him. "I wish I could do something for you," Anita spoke, her eyes still swimming.

Zack managed a twisted grin. "I've been in worse shape and survived," he said. "You ought to have seen me after I tried to ride a Longhorn bull on a bet down at the ranch."

The saddled horses were brought up, the same mounts on which they had been brought to this place. The Tollivers were freed from their chairs, and lifted onto mounts and tied there. The Ax produced a key, freed Zack from the leg irons, then prodded him into mounting the black gelding. His arms remained tied, and the Ogallala Kid and Matt Pecos helped lift him into the saddle. His ankles were lashed tight beneath the horse's belly. The cavalcade set off in the darkness.

"Where are you taking us?" Anita demanded.

"Back to whar you come from."

"Back to Sioux Wells?" she asked dubiously.

"O' course not. I mean we're takin' you back to that

fancy car you was holed up in. You ladies like that sort o' thing don't you? Fuss an' feathers. We aim to make you comfortable."

The Tollivers became silent, puzzled. Zack finally spoke to Julia. "How are you making out?"

"Instead o' frettin' about me you ought to be blamin' us for what happened to you," she said exhaustedly. "It was me that sent Hickok to talk you into joinin' these devils, usin' that cattle money as bait. Please forgive me. It was Frank Niles that really put me up to it. I never knew that he'd been waitin' a chance to kidnap me an' 'Nita an' force us to sign that order to his brother."

"I'm tellin' you people for the last time to keep quiet," The Ax snarled. He brought his horse alongside and whipped the muzzle of his pistol across Zack's face. The blow did little more than bruise and scrape the skin, but it brought a new streak of blood to add to the damage Zack had sustained.

He would have struck again, but Anita Tolliver managed to knee her horse near and lean far enough from the saddle to take the glancing blow on her shoulder. "Why be so cruel?" she implored. "What kind of a man are you?"

The Ax settled back in the saddle. He was a savage man in the habit of giving in to unbalanced emotions. "Next time I'll cut him to pieces," he frothed. "An' you too, if'n you git gay."

"At least do something for him," she sobbed. "Look at him! Burned, beaten. Why add to his suffering? You and your boss have got what you wanted haven't you?"

"He won't suffer much longer," The Ax said. "Neither will you."

That silenced her. If there had been any lingering hope in the minds of any of them that they might be allowed to live, it faded. The Ax was deadly, capable of more torture. Murder would be very easy on his conscience.

Julia Tolliver began to weep softly. "Be quiet!" The Ax snarled. "Next one that whimpers will be without a tongue."

He had a skinning knife in his hand. He meant what he said. Julia Tolliver still had the courage to look up into the sky and say, "Lord, have mercy on us. We're in the hands of demons."

They rode slowly. The Ax was apparently wasting time for some reason of his own. Although they had traveled this route in darkness the previous night Zack saw outcrops against the stars that, with a cattleman's mind for recording landmarks, he remembered. They were heading in the direction of the spot where the engine and palace car had been halted on the abandoned spur.

He glimpsed the single window light that marked the location of Box Springs Ranch again reminding him that the hunting lodge and shack where they had been held was within easy distance of the main outlaw stronghold.

Within less than an hour at the slogging pace The Ax demanded, they reached the abandoned track—the Crown Point spur, Julia had termed it. The smell of coal smoke was in the air. The Ax called a halt. Zack and the Tollivers were freed from the ropes that bound them to the horses and dragged to the ground. They were pushed roughly down a descent into the cut where the engine and palace car stood.

The engine was being manned by its crew. The boiler was being stoked and the steam boxes were alive. The engineer was at his seat in the cab, but he did not look out as The Ax moved past with the captives and the two gunmen.

The palace car was dark. Zack and the Tollivers, their arms bound, were pushed up the steps and marched into the lounge section. The Ax produced his bull's-eye lantern,

and also more thongs for bonds. The thongs were used
to lash the three captives securely to heavy swivel chairs
whose bases were fastened to the floor.

"All right, you two," The Ax said to the Kid and
Matt Pecos. "Go to the ranch. I'll be along later. Leave
my horse and talk to nobody about what you've seen
or where we've been."

The pair left the car and Zack presently heard them
riding away, leading the unneeded horses.

"You're going to kill us, aren't you?" Anita spoke.
Her voice was steady.

"Not me, miss," The Ax answered in pretended horror. "You're just goin' to start on your way up the line
again."

Although the car retained the stuffy heat of the day,
The Ax piled wood and scrap papers into a brass heating
stove that served the car in cold weather. He dashed on
some kerosene from a tin, struck a match and the stove
roared into life. He stood by pretending to briskly rub
his hands together against an imaginary chill. "Nothin'
like a warm fire to make a man happy," he remarked.

In the glow from the doors of the stove Zack saw
that three or four more five-gallon tins of kerosene had
been brought into the car and were standing dangerously
close to the roaring stove.

"Now wouldn't it be a shame if'n this here special got
to runnin' wild an' didn't make the curve at the bottom
of Rincon Hill?" The Ax said.

The man was looking at them with a death's-head grin.
He was torturing them, telling them their fate, enjoying
it. They were to be sent to their death in a wrecked train
which would burn and destroy all evidence that they
had been murdered.

"Bill Hickok will pay you off for this, Axel," Julia
Tolliver said hoarsely. "There won't be a hole deep

enough for you to hide in once he takes after you. You know him."

"Hickok won't be alive long enough to pay off anybody," The Ax grinned. "He'll be taken care of the minute he shows up tomorrow in Sioux Wells. We've got fellers in the bunch who'd enjoy puttin' a slug in his back. He's been kind of rough on some of 'em here an' there along the line."

The Ax closed the shutter on the lantern and they heard him leaving the car, heard his boots grind the gravel as he moved ahead toward the engine, which he boarded.

There was a faint refrain of conversation. Evidently Hank, the engineer, seemed to be debating a point. Zack heard The Ax cursing him and giving orders.

With a jolt, their car ground into motion. The engine and car were being backed down the spur, returning to the main line.

Zack strained wildly at his bonds. He failed. He could not escape. Anita and her grandmother burst into frenzy also, fighting to free themselves. That was also futile and the three of them were forced to fall back, exhausted.

"Where is this place The Ax mentioned?" Zack panted. "This Rincon Hill."

"Not far," Julia said dully. "Not far enough. 'Twon't take long to git there once we're on the main line. It's two miles of downgrade an' at the bottom there's a curve with a rock wall on one side called Castle Gate an' a gully on the other that's usually filled with dry brush an' driftwood at this time o' year. These devils figured it out good. If we go into the ditch that kerosene will go up like a volcano. We'll all burn, even these ropes they've tied us with. It'll look like an accident."

They again fought the bonds, but Zack only felt the knots grow tighter, threatening to entirely cut off circulation in his arms and legs. They were finally forced to give it up, lungs heaving.

The train slowed, jolted over switch frogs, then came to a stop. "Main line," Julia said.

There was silence for a time, except for the throbbing of the steam boxes. Then two pistol shots sounded. They looked at each other questioningly, but had no answer to what the gunplay meant.

Presently the drive wheels began to spin as though an inexperienced hand had yanked open the throttle. Their car rocked unevenly ahead. The locomotive wheels found more traction and the car began to roll faster, more smoothly. Zack heard the crunch of gravel and was sure that it meant that The Ax had leaped from the moving engine.

Their car rolled faster. Zack again made an agonized effort to break free. He managed to rip the swivel chair from its moorings and he toppled on his face on the thick carpet, the chair still bound to him. He was in a more helpless position than ever.

"It's no use," Julia said, and now her voice was calm. "Make our peace with the Lord. We've only got a few more minutes to live. We can only give our souls over to the mercy of—"

She broke off. Zack realized they were not alone in the car. A figure stood over him. "Stay quiet," a voice husked. "I've got a knife. I'm tryin' to cut you free."

"Gertie!" Julia Tolliver gasped. "Dear God, where did you come from?"

"No time for that," the husky voice said. Zack now recognized the arrival in the glow from the stove. She was the coarse-voiced, loud-talking dance-hall woman, Gussie Bluebell.

She was using a carving knife she evidently had got from the pantry. "Hurry!" she husked. "Stop that engine before we all git killed!"

Zack found himself free. The car was gaining speed. He ran to the front platform and mounted at frantic speed the iron ladder that reached the tender. He stumbled past the hatch of the water tank, and plunged to the floor of the cab amid an avalanche of coal.

He had a working knowledge of the operation of railway engines, having spent time with engine crews during switching operations at cattle shipping points.

He leaped at the figure that sat in the engineer's seat on the right side of the cab. He expected battle and his hands grasped for the throat. What he seized was a dead man. The corpse slumped from the seat and he saw the bullet wound and the fresh blood. The engineer had been shot in the back of the head. The fireman was slumped on the opposite seat. He too had been murdered. Undoubtedly they had been members of the outlaw organization. They were the men who had manned the engine the previous night. And undoubtedly they had been killed by The Ax to silence them as witnesses to the murder of the Tollivers.

Zack grasped the lever to reverse the drive wheels. The heavy lever did not move. He discovered that the crowbar the fireman used to loosen coal in the tender had been wedged into the slot in which the lever moved.

He yanked desperately at the crowbar, but it had been jammed too tightly in place. He had no time to labor over it. There was only one other hope. He knew that he could have leaped from the cab at that time and, with luck, emerged with no more than bruises. But there were the three in the lounge car. Julia Tolliver, in particular, would likely never survive such an effort.

He scrambled back over the tender and leaped to the platform of the parlor car. Gussie Bluebell had freed the Tollivers and all three of them were on the platform. He landed among them. The car, like all passenger cars, had the wheel of the handbrake on the platform.

"We've got to uncouple!" he panted. "I can't stop the engine! Help me! Start turning that hand brake!"

He vaulted the railing, pulled the coupling pin by its chain and yanked the lever that parted the jaws of the couplings.

Anita and her grandmother, being railroad people, had already grasped the idea and were frantically turning the iron brake wheel. For a moment there was no result. Then, the locomotive, its stack thudding faster each second, drew clear.

Zack leaped to the brake wheel, replacing Julia, and put his greater strength to the task. For heart-freezing seconds he feared that it was too late and that the car had gained too much momentum to be checked in time.

The car slowed suddenly. The engine pulled ahead and the car continued to lose speed. Wheels groaned and chattered, but the brakes were taking effect. The locomotive faded into the starlight ahead and Zack saw open track lengthening between it and the car.

The sagebrush slid past sluggishly now. There came a screeching of tortured metal ahead, then a heavy, booming crash. The engine, now more than a quarter of a mile ahead, had reached the curve at the foot of the Rincon and had plunged into the ravine.

Their own vehicle had slowed to a respectable pace, but was still drifting ahead. Zack kicked in place the ratchet that held the brake. "We've got to jump!" he panted. He indicated Anita Tolliver. "You first."

Without hesitation she descended the steps, poised a moment, then leaped. The pace was still a trifle fast, and Zack saw her stumble and sprawl.

"You!" he said to Gussie Bluebell. "Land running and you'll be all right."

But Gussie, not as young nor as experienced with trains as Anita, fell when her feet touched the ground.

Zack turned and kicked free the brake ratchet. The wheel spun violently as the brakes were released.

Julia Tolliver was already on the steps, ready to leave the car. "I kin make it," she said.

But Zack pushed past her, dropped to the ground and caught her as she followed him. They both fell, but he managed to twist so that he took the brunt of it.

"Dang it, I could have made it better by myself," she complained, scrambling to her feet. "I was hoppin' trains afore you was born."

Zack had picked up a few more bruises and had lost some cuticle. Anita and Gussie Bluebell came scrambling to join them. They also were nursing skinned hands and knees and had torn clothing, but all of them had come out of it without broken bones.

The car, gaining speed again, vanished into the darkness. A heavy explosion sounded down the grade. The boiler of the ditched engine had exploded.

Then came a new grinding crash. The palace car had left the rails and plunged into the ravine. A burst of flame rose, turned into a fireball that floated majestically higher. The kerosene had ignited from the wrecked stove.

"There goes five thousand dollars' worth o' rollin' stock," Julia Tolliver moaned. "An' me an' 'Nita as poor as church mice. Why did you wreck it, cowboy?"

"I'm trying to make them believe we're all dead," Zack said. "If we had left that car sitting on the track they'd be after us as fast as you can wink. I'm not too sure they won't be suspicious anyway because there were two wrecks instead of one. In any event we're a long way from being out of the woods. The Ax and those two leppies who are his heel dogs will likely do some scouting to make sure things went their way."

"My husband had that purty car built 'special for me as a weddin' present years ago," Julia sighed.

"Keep your voices down," Zack cautioned. "I tell you—"

His warning had come none too soon. He heard the sounds of hoofs in the night. He pushed Julia and the two younger women down, and they flattened in the weeds alongside the track.

By this time the fire below the grade had grown to a giant torch that lighted up the flats and ridges around them. They flattened still more. Evidently the dead brush in the ravine was adding to the blaze. The riders came nearer.

Chapter 10

The padding of hoofs passed by, and Zack chanced a glance. Two riders, rifles jutting from saddle slings, were moving past. They were lax and hipshot in the hulls—the posture of men who believed they were wasting time. They were so close Zack recognized them. The Ogallala Kid and Matt Pecos. Zack crouched back again and waited until all sounds had died. The course of the two desperadoes indicated that they were heading for Box Springs Ranch.

He lifted to his knees, listening. The Ax was still to be accounted for. But, after a time, he decided that there was no immediate danger from that source.

He spoke to Gussie Bluebell. "Now, where in blazes did you drop from? Why and how?"

"Her real name ain't Gussie Bluebell," Julia said. "It's Gertrude Hanson. She's an old friend of mine. She was cookin' fer one of our gradin' crews when we was buildin' the Rocky west into Sioux Wells."

"She will always be Gussie Bluebell to me," Zack said. "But how—?"

"I work in a dance hall these days, fer there ain't been any cookin' jobs open since the Rocky had to stop buildin' west," Gussie said. "I don't claim to be an example of refinement, but I ain't as bad as some folk think. An' I don't forget my friends. Mrs. Tolliver, here, has done me some big favors in the past. She always had treated me like a lady, an' she pulled me through some bad spots when I needed help. I never had any hand in

139

what these highbinders was doin', but I had eyes an' ears. I overheard Lila an' that scoundrel, Jim Axel, whisperin' together a few nights ago. I didn't git the drift of it, but somethin' big was in the wind, an' I heard the Tollivers mentioned. I knew it meant harm to Julia an' Anita, so I tipped off Bill Hickok to warn them that it might be better if they got out of Sioux Wells."

"Hickok wouldn't tell us where the warning came from," Anita said. "He probably was afraid the outlaws might find out and take it out on you."

"But how did you get into that car?" Zack asked.

"It was that buffalo hunter, Ed Hake," Gussie said. "He likes to rile me up with things like shootin' holes in the water tank, but we're old friends. He had heard rumors there was a big herd of buffalo out in the direction of the old Crown Point spur an' rode out there to take a look-see. He didn't find any sign o' buffalo. I was havin' a beer with him an' he mentioned that he'd sighted J. K. Tolliver's private car an' an engine spotted on the spur. He thought it was a little odd. So did I, for I knew the Tollivers had pulled out the night before on the fancy car. Hickok had told me so. They should have been in Junction City an' headin' east. It didn't smell right to me, so I hired a horse an' buggy at the livery this afternoon, sayin' I was just goin' for a ride. I headed for the Crown Point sidin', an' got there at dark. When I found they was gittin' up steam, I decided I'd wait it out. So I tied up the horse an' rig an' sneaked aboard, figurin' somethin' would turn up sooner or later. An' it did."

"Oh, Gertie, how can I tell you how grateful we air," Julia said, and kissed the dance-hall woman. "You know what will happen to you if they find out what you did."

"I know," Gussie said. "But they got to ketch me first. I knew somethin' bad had happened to you an' Anita when I saw how your clothes was strewn around your staterooms. I got a .32 an' I figure that I might be killed, but I might take some of them skunks with me."

Anita also kissed Gussie and hugged her. "We would all be down there, burned to death, if you hadn't risked your life for us," she said.

"I don't like to mention this," Zack said, "but I've got a sort of feeling up my backbone that by this time The Ax is beginning to really wonder why the car was ditched minutes after the engine. Come daybreak he might have a lot of people looking for sign of anyone who might be wandering around this country. They've probably got lookouts stationed on the hills around Box Springs to keep track of anything that moves, such as us. The Ax might not even wait for daybreak if he starts adding two and two."

"Daybreak ain't too fur away," Granny Tolliver said. "We better hole up. This country's full o' gullies an' brush."

"Hickok!" Zack said, and let it ride there.

They all peered at him, a new freezing chill on them. "You heard what The Ax said," Zack went on. "Hickok is marked to be killed, and they likely won't waste any time. They're out to wipe out all witnesses, even among their own outfit. Hickok has got to be warned—and fast."

He looked up at the stars. As Julia had said, the night was well along. "Where are we?" he asked. "How far are we from Sioux Wells?"

Julia answered that. "The Crown Point spur is fifteen miles out," she said. "We're a couple of miles or more beyond it now. I'd say eighteen miles." She added spunkily, "We ain't never goin' to git there by standin' around here talkin' about it. Let's git movin'. Eighteen miles ain't much fer healthy, spry people. I've walked a lot farther'n that in a day, an' drove a six-horse team an' a load o' crossties in the bargain."

They set out, Zack leading the way. They moved along

in silence for a space. Granny Julia finally broke that lull. "What I need is about a gallon of water all in one gulp," she said. "I'm so thirsty I could even enjoy alkali gyp water."

"And a nice big steak with fried spuds, apple pie and a slab of cheese," Zack said. "It just occurred to me it's been a long time between meals."

Anita moved in and pretended to stamp on his foot—but lightly. "Won't you ever learn not to provoke me?" she said.

They came presently to a small seep of water. It was fairly fresh, and they reveled in it for minutes, dousing their heads, satisfying their parched tongues. After that they moved along almost light-heartedly, carrying with them the belief that they had risen from the grave.

"When we git to town we'll put a crimp in Frank Niles an' his brother," Julia said as she trudged along over the rough going. "An' put them both in the pen."

"Would those papers you signed be legal?" Zack asked.

"Not when we kin prove duress," Julia said. "But they figgered it out mighty slick. The paper they forced us to sign was dated the day we got back to Sioux Wells. That was the same day you got mixed up in things. We're supposed to be dead. There will be plenty of witnesses, honest people, who will testify that we was friendly with Frank Niles that day, an' not actin' like we suspected him of anythin'. Fact is, we wasn't. Except for Niles an' Bill Hickok, there's nobody but them two on the engine crew who knew we left Sioux Wells on that special last night an' not tonight. As fur as folks know, we was killed in a train wreck. There'll be no evidence of us havin' been tied up, fer the fire will destroy all that sort of evidence. Them two that was on the engine won't tell the truth, bein' as they acted like they was highbinders too."

"They'll never tell," Zack said. "They're dead. The

Ax killed them before he started the engine running wild. Their skeletons in the fire would only be taken as further evidence the wreck was accidental."

That brought gasps of horror. "They're even killin' their own kind to protect themselves," Julia moaned.

Anita spoke. "We can't think of trying to walk to Sioux Wells. We couldn't possibly make it until late in the morning. By that time it would be too late. That devil, The Ax, said Hickok would be killed as soon as he appears in town this morning."

Zack turned to Julia. "A train? Won't there be a train along that we can stop?"

She shook her head dolefully. "Ain't nothin' scheduled eastbound out of the Wells until ten in the mornin'. The last eastbound went by before The Ax had our car backed off the spur. He made sure of that. It was why he dallied around so long before puttin' us on the main line."

"Westbound?" Zack asked hopefully.

"There'll be a passenger due along about eight o'clock, but it won't be able to git past the Castle Gate wreck," Julia said.

"Won't they be sending out a work train from the Wells to clean up the wreck?" Zack said.

"Likely they don't know about it," Julia said. "The telegraph line probably is burned out at Castle Gate."

Zack whirled on Gussie, snapping his fingers. "How stupid can I get," he exclaimed. "Your livery rig! Where did you leave it?"

"I tied up the horse in a gully near the place where I found out the engine and the Tolliver car was standin'," she said.

"We've got to find it," Zack said. "You ladies, at least, can make it to the Wells, maybe in time to warn Hickok."

They surged ahead faster, buoyed by new hope. Zack stayed with Julia as they made their way at as fast a pace as possible through the brush and outcrops, their shoes sinking into the loose, shifting soil of the plains. They were not always successful in avoiding obstacles. They often stumbled, or went sprawling, tripped by roots and gopher holes that threatened them with sprained ankles. Once, disturbed rattlesnakes sounded their fearsome shrilling, freezing them in their tracks, causing them to slowly backtrack and circle far wide of the area.

Julia began to fail. Zack swung her to his shoulder and swung along in the wake of Gussie and Anita. "I kin make it," she wailed. "Put me down."

"You'll get your chance," Zack told her. "I'm not of a mind to pack you all the way into the Wells."

The weed-grown spur track appeared abruptly out of the darkness across their path. "Here we are!" Gussie said exultantly. "It must be west of us where I left the horse an' buggy. It can't be too far."

Enlivened they moved along at a fast gait. Even Julia's frail weight was telling on Zack when he suddenly called a halt. "Listen!" he breathed.

They could hear faint, far sounds in the windless stillness. They were rough voices, profane voices. Zack was certain he made out the rasping tones of The Ax, angry and fuming.

"We're too late," he whispered. "They've found Gussie's livery rig. Now they really can add two and two and figure out that we must have had help and are probably alive and on foot."

They retreated, freezing disappointment replacing their eagerness. They left the railroad spur and headed northward through the open brush. There was no sign of immediate pursuit. Hope began to grow in them again, but Zack was sure The Ax would guess that they would have attempted to reach the livery rig, and would eventually decide they had been warned away.

However the country was big, vast. Hope grew that

they might escape under cover of darkness. They were following the pointers on the Big Dipper which marked the North Star, for in that direction lay Sioux Wells. But daybreak was now little more than an hour away.

"We'll never make it in time to save him," Gussie finally said in a flat voice.

"We'll make it," Anita said. "You think a lot of Bill Hickok, don't you?"

"There was a time some years ago when I was cookin' for the U.P. an' Bill was scoutin' for the Army that we talked about maybe gittin' ourselves a claim an' settlin' down," Gussie said. "I was younger then, an' wasn't bad lookin', even if I do say it myself. But it didn't turn out that way. I never forgot how we talked an' dreamed. An' I know he's never forgot. He told me just lately he wished things hadn't turned out the way they did for him. Whether we git there today in time won't make much difference in the long run for him. Some day he'll be shot —likely in the back. He knows it, I know it. It's the way men like him die. Death has always followed him."

"We can't give up," Anita said. "We've *got* to get there in time and warn him."

They were driven now by a determination that overcame weariness and weakness. Julia seemed to have been rejuvenated, and insisted on walking on her own feet the greater part of the time, submitting to being assisted by Gussie and Anita at times, or carried over some of the harder going on Zack's shoulder. At times she hopped agilely along over obstacles, setting a pace that was almost too much for the others.

"It was me that brung Bill Hickok into the Wells," she said once. "If'n he's murdered, it'll haunt me to my grave. He only took the job as a favor to me."

Anita tripped over some hidden snare and fell. Zack lifted her to her feet. She looked up at him, then reached up, and tenderly stroked his cheek with her fingertips.

He kissed her and she clung to him for a space, wordlessly.

Then they hurried on. The hope grew brighter in Zack with each passing minute. There was now the possibility they might build up distance that could not be overcome even if their trail was cut at daybreak.

Then they heard the dogs. The sound was far away, coming to them over dark distances, but it was unmistakable. Julia uttered a small despairing sigh. Anita moved closer to Zack and took his hand. She was trembling.

Zack was remembering the sounds of kenneled dogs that he had heard while he was at Box Springs Ranch. He feared that he now heard the occasional tolling bell voice of a bloodhound amid the screeching of the pack.

Gussie, weeping, began to run, but Zack caught her by the arm. "No! Easy! The dogs haven't cut our trail yet. They're only circling and yipping. They're mainly catch dogs, trained to trail horses, but there might be a hound among them. The hound doesn't act like he's on the scent either. When they pick up what they want they'll settle down to steady screeching. The hound will say nothing."

"There's one thing I want understood," Gussie said. "I ain't lettin' them take me alive. That man, Axel, ain't human. He likes to torture an' see folks suffer. My gun is only a .32 but it'll serve the purpose." She looked at Julia and Anita. "An' I advise you to decide the same."

She had produced a short-muzzled weapon from somewhere. "Never mind thinking about anything like that," Zack said. "Maybe you better give me that gun."

"Only if an' when I figure you're goin' to need it worse than us ladies," Gussie said.

They pushed ahead as fast as the terrain permitted. The sounds of pursuit had died. But that proved to be only a trick of the wind. The clamor of the dogs came again, louder, nearer. They had picked up the trail, but they were still a long distance behind them—a mile or more, Zack judged.

They came upon a wide stream bed with a rushing creek in its midst. They fell gratefully into the cold water, slaking their thirst. The yammer of the dogs was undeniably closer now. They followed the stream, wading often to their waists, fighting against the rush of water. They kept this up for exhausting minute after minute, hoping to at least throw the pursuit off for a time.

They found themselves confronted by a cascade where the creek plunged down a twenty-foot drop. Zack carried Julia up that water-greased ascent over rocks on which he somehow found foothold. Gussie and Anita followed him and it was sheer will and desperation that brought them to the top where the creek leveled and flowed gently through mounded sandbars.

Zack staggered upstream for a time, with Julia clinging to him, then fell, utterly spent, on a sandbar. Julia, weeping and crooning over him, brushed the hair back from his forehead. "An' to think that it was me that brought not only Hickok into all this, but you too, cowboy," she sobbed.

Anita and Gussie had sunk down also, too spent to go on for the moment at least. They lay there, listening. They could hear the dogs far in the distance. The sounds became confused, fading, rising, fading, rising again. Finally silence.

"They've lost us," Zack finally decided. "It's my guess they're covering both sides of the creek downstream, figuring we would head in that direction rather than go against the current. But they'll swing this way before long."

They finally took to the stream again, taking advantage of the easier going through the flats. An old sickle moon was in the sky now, giving faint light.

"Wasn't it me that was so thirsty I said I could drink a river dry a little while ago?" Julia croaked. "The Lord sometimes provides too much." In spite of the milder current she was able to progress only by constant help from Zack or the girls.

Zack saw that Anita and Gussie were also nearing their limit. In the faint moonlight he saw a ledge near at hand that rose twenty feet or more from the water's edge. It appeared to be part of an outcrop that extended some distance north of the stream.

"All right," he said hoarsely. "We'll try it here."

Standing in a pool to his waist, he lifted Granny Julia to a foothold. The ledge was broken and fissured so that Julia was equal to the occasion. She found a new reservoir of strength and climbed upward. Zack mounted just below her, ready to catch her if she fell. The two girls followed close below him.

They all scrambled safely to a broad ledge and sank down to regain their strength. Now that they were away from the babble of the stream, they again could hear the distant yelping of the dogs. Zack said nothing. The dogs were still circling, but they were casting the area along the stream, heading in their direction once again.

They huddled together, listening, waiting. The sounds of the chase bore relentlessly down upon them. Zack placed an arm round Julia Tolliver, drawing her against him. She was quivering, but still brave. She sighed and murmured, "It's been a mighty long time since I let a man cuddle me."

Another head leaned against Zack's shoulder. Anita. She remained there for comfort and courage. Gussie Bluebell sat like a statue, her small pistol in her hand—alone as she had fought her way through life.

The yapping of the dogs became more distinct. Zack found one note of hope. The deep voice of the bloodhound sounded only intermittently. The dog was keeping its whereabouts known, but Zack was certain it was grow-

ing tired and disinterested. Their battle upstream had
left no scent for the animal to pick up.

Presently, they made out the approach of riders, and
finally heard an occasional voice as men called to each
other.

The dogs, the horses, the voices, moved past. The
sounds faded into the mellow, faint moonlight. Zack began to breathe more deeply. He felt the Tollivers quivering
more violently. Gussie bowed her head and uttered a
prayer of deliverance.

Chapter 11

"We're safe now, aren't we?" Anita said. She was forcing conviction into her voice, more for her grandmother's sake and the rest of them than for herself.

"Of course," Zack said. But he knew better, and he was aware that so did she. But, at least they had gained time—many minutes at least, and perhaps much longer before the searchers swung back to again circle the area.

"We can't stay here," he said. He looked at Julia. "Where are we in relation to the railroad? How far?"

"I'd say two miles," she said. "East of us." Then she uttered a little cry of self-condemnation. "If'n I ain't a fool! The Sand Crick sidin'. It ought to be somewhere about directly east of us if'n I'm thinkin' halfway straight."

"The Sand Creek siding? What good will—?"

"It's a sidetrack for layin' over work trains an' such," Julia explained. "There's a tool shack there an' there might be a handcar to be had. It would be a lot better and faster than walkin' all the way to the Wells—even if the highbinders wasn't around to scoop us up."

Enlivened by hope once again, they stumbled their way out of the outcrop and reached more level ground. They found themselves in a devil's garden of sharp-fanged boulders that jutted like the fins of sharks through the surface, which was soft and was certain to leave footprints.

Heavy clouds blotted out the moon and stars. A chill wind assailed them—their garments still wet from the

150

stream. The wind opposed them, as had the stream. They bent against it, moving into its teeth. It moaned and whistled along the brush, and some of those sounds came not from the wind but from the throats of coyotes who were seizing this chance to pounce on prairie dogs and jack rabbits under cover of the drive of the storm.

Julia said brokenly, "God, why have You forsaken us?"

The faint moon began playing tag with scattering clouds, and in that elusive light Zack kept peering ahead, but all that loomed were more hummocks of grass, more patches of brush, more needlerocks—more distance.

"I never figured I'd be so anxious to see a train track again after all the grief one caused me," he mumbled as they were all forced to pause and rest.

They wandered into a prairie dog village and worked their way among mounds and treacherous burrows without meeting new disaster.

Anita spoke in a strangled voice. "Look!"

Telegraph poles loomed close at hand, linked by the gossamer threads of wires. They saw the rise of the embankment, studded with the ends of crossties. They had reached the main line of the Rocky Mountain Express.

"Forgive me, Oh Lord, for doubting You," Julia said.

Zack halted, motioning for silence. He stood, listening, combing the night for sound. The wind brought nothing but the sighing and complaining of the brush.

"This Sand Creek sidetrack?" he asked Julia. "Which direction would it be?"

"I just don't know," she said exhaustedly. "I cain't pick out any landmarks to tell me where we air. It might be south of us, it might be north. One thing I'm sure, it ain't fur away."

"Sioux Wells is north of us," Zack said. "We might as well take a chance and try in that direction. At least we won't be losing any distance if we have to make it all the way on foot."

They stumbled along the ties. They were moving mechanically now, with Zack again carrying Julia the major part of the time.

Dawn was pink in the sky when Zack saw a shape looming up ahead. Anita saw it also and uttered a little sighing sound. "The siding," she mumbled. "Sand Creek. And there's the tool shack."

"And, glory be, there's the handcar standin' alongside the shack if my eyes ain't deceivin' me," Julia exclaimed. "We'll now have wheels under us. Railroad wheels. It ain't hard goin' from here into the Wells, mainly level with only a couple of rises to pump over, an' then some downgrade the last couple o' miles into town."

It was then they again heard the dogs. The sound was brought from a distance by the wind. It faded, but rose again. Pursuit was coming up—and fast.

They raced to the shack. The handcar, which was propelled by manually-operated bars that turned cogs and wheels, stood on the travel ramp alongside the shack, where it had been left overnight by the section hands.

With the sounds of pursuit growing in their ears, they desperately seized the vehicle, intending to set it on the rails. It was made of good railroad iron and strong lumber and very heavy. Even so, their desperate efforts began to move it.

But only a foot or two. Then they stopped. They discovered that it was secured to a ringbolt in the tool shed by a stout length of chain, and padlocked.

They halted, panting. "There'll be tools in the shanty to bust the padlock," Julia gasped. "Sledges, crowbars."

But the shanty was also padlocked. Gussie pushed her pistol into Zack's hands. "Blow it off," she said.

Zack knew the sound would carry to the oncoming pursuers. Then he blew off the padlock with two shots. Hurling the door open he scrabbled around in the interior and found a sledge hammer. Emerging, he smashed the padlock that linked the chain, freeing the handcar.

They once more strained at the vehicle. They could now hear the hammering hoofs of the horses as the chase came up. The gunshots had been heard, and the pursuers knew that their quarry was near.

With Zack using a crowbar that he had taken from the tool shack, they inched the heavy car astride the rails. He was prying the flanged wheels into place when Julia uttered a despairing cry. "We're too late! They're upon us!"

Zack made out the shape of oncoming riders. Screeching dogs came out of the darkness to surround them, snarling and darting at them in pretended attack.

He got the wheels in place on the rails, felt the vehicle move freely. He lifted Julia onto the car. "All aboard!" he panted. "Get pumping!"

Julia already was straining at the bars with her frail strength. Anita and Gussie joined her. Zack remained on the ground, digging his heels against the crossties, putting his shoulder against the car, veins bulging in his forehead as he strained to force the ponderous weight into motion.

The wheels began to turn—slowly, agonizingly. They creaked and grated on the rails. The cogs protested with metallic groaning. With dogs snarling at his heels, their teeth clashing, Zack strained harder.

A voice shouted, "They're tryin' to git away on a handcar!"

That voice belonged to The Ax. Zack found the strength for supreme effort. The bars were beginning to rise and fall faster as inertia was overcome. Zack leaped aboard and put his strength to the bars.

A gun opened up, then another. The flashes were lurid in the dawn. Zack heard the sullen buzz of a spent bullet, for the range was long for a pistol. Another spent slug struck metal on the handcar and dropped at Zack's feet.

He fired one shot from Gussie's pistol in reply, but only

for effect, for he knew it was wasted as far as finding any human target was concerned. The handcar was moving faster now with each rise and fall of the bars. The landscape began to slide past at an unexpected pace. Zack realized they were on a downgrade and the handcar was beginning to run out of control. The bars were whipping up and down so violently they were being nearly torn from the grasp of the four passengers.

"How do you slow this thing down?" he shouted.

"Step on the brake!" Julia panted. "It's that pedal on your side. Don't you cowpokes know anythin'? Hurry, before we go flyin' into the ditch! But careful, too, or you'll derail us! Easy does it!"

Zack found the brake and tried to get their careening vehicle under control. "Hang on!" he gritted. For a freezing space he thought he had failed and that the handcar was going to leave the rails under the grip of the brake. Then it held to the track and began to slow. And just in time, for the flanges screeched wildly as the car rounded a curve. But the wheels clung to the rails. Then they were on more level track.

All sounds of pursuit had been left far behind. Zack manned the bars again. Anita sat down weakly in the limited deck space, keeping her head clear of the bars. "I think I'm going to throw up," she stuttered faintly.

"Me too," Gussie groaned.

"Do it downwind, both of you," Julia commanded. "I'm surprised you kin find anythin' to throw. It's been so long since I had a bite to eat my stomach's wearin' itself out ag'in my backbone. You young ones ain't got a bit o' spunk."

Then she leaned over the side of the car and was sick herself. That seemed to be the tonic the younger pair needed, for they crept over to help her, then arose and manned the bars of the handcar with new strength, for their vehicle had found a slight upgrade and needed motive power now.

Zack felt a little limp himself, but it was Granny who drove that out of him. She recovered swiftly. "I guess it must have been somethin' I et a couple of days ago," she said, forcing herself to restore her brassy bravado.

Zack looked at the lightening sky. "As I judge it, we're still a dozen miles or so out of the Wells," he said. "It's going to take us up to two hours to make it, for this thing isn't what might be called a ball of fire. The sun will be up long before that."

"You mean you're afraid The Ax might catch up with us?" Anita asked apprehensively.

"There's not much chance of that," he said. "Not unless they've got fresh horses somewhere, which isn't likely. After all, those animals they had been riding were pretty well used up after a night's work. But you forget that there's a person in Sioux Wells named Frank Niles who will be even more anxious than The Ax to be the first to greet us. And he's got help. That's for sure."

They all knew what he meant. Not only Bill Hickok's life was at stake in the town now, but their own if they dared appear openly in broad daylight with Niles' gunmen waiting.

"Maybe Frank ain't in the Wells," Julia quavered. "Maybe he's hid out somewhere to make sure things will blow over."

"He's there," Zack said. "And waiting for us."

"How come?" Julia protested. "Maybe he don't even know we're alive. He might not—"

"He knows. And he knows by this time we're on our way on this handcar. You forget that telegraph line to the ranch I told you about. The Ax is sure to have sent someone to the ranch to warn Niles. They'll be waiting for us—and for Hickok. Niles has got everything to lose now, including his neck, if any of us are alive when the day is over, and he knows it."

"They'll be sendin' out a work train to clean up the wreck," Gussie burst out. "We kin stop an' wait. They won't be highbinders on the work train. They'll help us."

"I'd say that there won't be any wreck train called until Niles gives the word," Zack said. "After all, nobody is supposed to know about that wreck, and you can bet he's got one of his crooked telegraph operators on duty at the Wells."

They labored woodenly at the bars, drugged by exhaustion, weighed down by the fear that they were continuing a race they had no chance to win. Julia's small, delicate face was gray, drawn. Zack took her hands gently from the bars and said, "Lie down and rest. Don't you know when to quit?"

She sank down, too spent to spark a protest. Zack and the two girls put their own fading strength to the bars. They were opposed now by another of the slight upgrades and Zack knew their vehicle was slowing little by little in spite of their efforts.

"Just a little piece more," Anita mumbled. "We're near the top of the rise. "Then we can almost coast into the Wells."

The sun was peering over the horizon, flooding the hills around them with golden tints. Those hills remained silent, devoid of life except for birds of prey which were rising to soar the sky in search of morning meals.

The handcar slowed still more. The clanking of the cogs was weary. Zack slid off and began pushing. The two girls followed his example, feeling that they could better utilize their strength in that manner.

The handcar's stolid weight fought them now. It became a malevolent foe instead of a friendly ally that had carried them out of the grip of their pursuers.

Then Zack felt the weight lighten. The vehicle lost its

opposition, became alive again. Zack pushed Anita and Gussie aboard. They had reached the crest. Ahead, the track stretched straight as a ruler along a gentle downgrade toward a sprawling settlement some two miles ahead. Sioux Wells.

They clung to the handlebars, letting the vehicle coast, as they watched the town take shape. In the early sun Zack could make out the structures along Railroad Street, the water tanks on the roofs of the Good Time and Travler's Rest, the red-painted railroad station with its peaked second-floor roof. There were the railroad yards with boxcars, flats and slat cars idle on the sidings. Smoke lifted from the repair shops that flanked the sidetracks. A switch engine, miniature at that distance, moved among the yards. Workmen in dungarees and carrying lunchpails were walking to work.

"Looks normal," Zack said.

"Not exactly," Anita spoke. "They *are* making up a wreck train. The yard engine is pulling out the crane car. That means that Niles knows everything. The telegraph line is in operation."

The handcar was entering a cut whose rims hid the view of the town. "We better get off here," Zack said. "We'll be in plain sight if we roll on out into the open. Once Niles sights us they'll be watching. I will try to go in first to scout around and warn Hickok."

"Not a chance," Anita said. "I've got a better idea. First, we must ditch this jig car. If they've already sighted us, they'll likely be sitting tight, waiting for us to come rolling right into their arms. But I doubt if they've spotted us. We've got the sun right at our backs, and we're still a long way out. Follow me and do as I say."

They managed to move the unwieldy vehicle off the rails and let it roll down the embankment into the weeds.

"We need a friend now," Anita said, "and we Tollivers

still have some around here. They aren't all highbinders, not by a long shot."

Now that she had taken charge and was coming to grips with her foes she was all strength and determination. They followed at her heels as she led the way through brush and small ridges that still cut them off from possible observation of watchers in town.

They descended an embankment to the course of a small stream. Beyond the watercourse stood a small farm on a flat. The house was a patchwork, hip-roofed structure, its walls built of railroad ties and scrap lumber, its roof of sheet iron and tarpaper. It was flanked by a small, flourishing cornfield and a well-kept truck garden where beans and peas were luxuriant on poles. There were patches of cabbage, carrots and a potato field. The stream had been dammed with logs and an irrigation system devised.

Julia suddenly came to life after having followed her granddaughter dubiously. "Of course!" she exclaimed. "Of course! The Washburns! Why didn't I think of them?"

They waded knee-deep across the stream and ran toward the house. A small, black child, no more than four, who was playing with a wooden doll, fled in fear around the corner of the house, screaming for her mother.

Beyond the house a black man in linsey and cotton jeans was loading a rickety wagon with a canvas top with baskets of vegetables, fresh-picked. A mule was in harness. The black man seized up a shotgun that had been thrust inside the wagon and came running, the weapon ready. He raised the gun, then slowly lowered it, staring in growing amazement at these apparitions that had appeared on his farm.

"Glory, glory be!" he exclaimed. "That ain't you, is it Misses Tolliver? An' you, Missy 'Nita? You ain't ghosts ris' from the daid, are you?"

Zack could understand. He looked at the three female members of his party. Their hair hung long and stringy. Gussie's peroxide had faded. Julia was witchlike in her ragged, tattered, worn aspect. Only Anita seemed a vestige of her real self. She was still beautiful, pale, eyes sunken, but beautiful. As for himself, he could imagine the black man's consternation. Fragments of his shirt still hung from his belt. The blood had matted on the hair of his chest. One eye was nearly closed, and his face was puffed and colored with more dried blood.

"We're all alive, but we thought we were goners several times lately, Noah," Julia said. "Hide us. We're in deep trouble. The binders are after us to kill us. Frank Niles is their leader. We just found it out. Hide us until we can collect our wits."

A handsome, barefoot black woman in calico and sun-bonnet appeared. "Mattie!" Julia sobbed. She turned to Zack and Gussie. "These are the Washburns," she explained. "Old friends. Noah and Mattie Washburn. Gussie, you know them, of course. They also worked for us when we were building the Rocky. They settled here at the Wells and took up farming."

Mattie Washburn embraced Julia and Anita, and shook hands with Gussie. She led the way into the house. The small girl they had seen peeked cautiously at them from around a doorway. A baby of less than a year gurgled in a homemade crib, smiling happily up at Anita who moved to hover over the crib, saying things women say to babies. Zack saw filled washtubs at the rear of the house and clotheslines from which many garments dangled.

"Noah farms and peddles vegetables in town," Anita explained. "Mattie takes in washing. You can trust them."

Noah Washburn and his wife listened, wide-eyed as Anita hurriedly told their story. "I always knew thet slick-talkin' Frank Niles was crooked somewhere," Noah said.

"But I never knew he was all bad. Now, you all, jest keep hid here. I'll go into town an' sorta size up the situation."

Zack looked out at the vegetable wagon. The mule stood hipshot, idly switching at flies. "Have you got a gun?" he asked Noah. "A real hammerhead, I mean. One that knocks holes in things. This shooter I'm carrying is a lady's gun, and there's only a live shell or two in it. I haven't had time to check. I need something that packs more authority."

"All I got is this here scatter-gun," Noah said. "An' it's only loaded fer birds to keep eagles an' such off'n my hen roost."

"The .32 will have to do," Zack said. "I'm going into town with you. I've got to warn Bill Hickok that he's ticketed for over the hill. Let's go. I'll hide in your wagon. The ladies will stay here."

"Not this gal," Julia Tolliver said emphatically. "After goin' this far, I ain't of a mind to hide under a bed while you an' Bill Hickok take on Frank Niles an' his thugs."

Gussie Bluebell spoke. "I'll be needed too. I know what goes on in the Wells. Hickok will be gettin' up an' settin' out for the Good Time about this time for his mornin' pick-me-up, an' will then go over to the Delmonico for breakfast. I figure we might have an even chance of sneakin' into the Good Time by the backdoor. From my room you get a good view up an' down Railroad Street, an' maybe we kin git there in time. All the other girls will still be asleep at this hour. We can hide in Noah's wagon. But, hurry. We might be too late already."

Zack seized Gussie's arm and they ran out of the house. He lifted her into the rickety wagon and she squeezed among the fragrant baskets of vegetables. He started to climb in to join her, but was pushed aside.

It was Anita. "Do you think I'm going to let you go into that place alone?" she said. She scrambled past him into the wagon, and gave him a twisted smile. "Besides, Grandma and I can't stay here. If things went wrong and they found us here they'd take it out on Noah and Mattie."

Zack found himself again being pushed aside, this time by Julia who crowded herself into the wagon between the younger pair. "Git goin'!" Julia said.

Zack started to debate it, then realized that it would only be a waste of very precious time. He slid into the wagon, folding his long legs in the cramped quarters.

Noah arranged the ragged top to better cover them and brought a worn tarp to throw over them and the vegetables. "May de Good Lawd look after us," he said as he climbed into the seat. "Now, you gals keep as quiet as though you was daid. I got a feelin' there's goin' to be big trouble in Sioux Wells before this mawnin' is over, an' thet somebody is goin' to be really daid! Let's hope it ain't none of us."

He mounted the seat and released the brake. He slapped the reins on the mule's back. The mule leaned into the collar, then, surprised by the unexpected weight, looked around reproachfully at Noah. Noah lifted the whip from the socket and brandished it threateningly. "Git along, you lazy scamp," he said. "For once, you are goin' to earn your keep."

The mule heaved a sigh and buckled down to the task. The wagon lurched along on crooked wheels over the chuckhole path out of the Washburn farm and onto the main wagon road that led toward the outlying shacks and farms around the town.

Zack found an eyehole in the weathered top and followed their progress. The wagon jolted across a spur track, creaked deeper into the town and turned up a weedy alleyway at the rear of the business structures which fronted on Railroad Street.

The sun was now high enough to beat down on the

canvas within inches of his head and he became aware again of the need for food and water—food above all.

"See anything out of the ordinary, Noah?" he whispered.

"Sure do," the driver murmured. "Dar's a man on de roof of de hotel, hidin' under de watah tank. He got a rifle. I see him clearer now. He is one o' de highbinders. Name of Buck Anders. A bad one. He's killed two men here in de Wells in saloon brawls. He takes apples an' peaches off'n my wagon, an' laughs at me when I ask him to pay. An' dar's another one up in de loft o' de barn at Tim Sullivan's livery yard. I jest got a peek at him as he leaned out to signal to de one on de hotel. He's got a rifle. I'd say de marshal, glory be to de Lawd, ain't showed up yet, an' dey're still waitin' fer him."

The vehicle was approaching the rear of the Good Time. "Anybody else in sight?" Zack whispered.

"Cain't see a soul," Noah breathed. "I'll stop as close to the door o' the Good Time as possible, an' give the word if the coast is still clear so you folks kin slip inside."

The wagon halted. Noah uttered a word of caution, and they remained rigidly silent while the steps of a passer-by approached and continued on down the alley.

"Now!" Noah whispered. Zack alighted, lifting Julia and the younger pair down. Gussie opened the door, made sure the coast was clear and they crowded in.

"This way," Gussie breathed and led the way up a stairway that was enclosed, shutting off the view of the bar and gambling room. They reached a hallway on the second floor, with the doors of several rooms to their left. They tiptoed in Gussie's wake toward the front.

One of the doors opened, and the disheveled, sleepy face of a girl appeared there. Her eyes widened in surprise, then in consternation. Gussie placed a hand against the girl's eyes and pushed her back into the room. "See nothin', hear nothin', dearie, an' you'll live to a ripe old age," she said.

She led the way to a door at the far end of the hall, tried the knob, and to her relief, it was unlocked. She ushered them into a room that was evidently larger than most, with a bed, two easy chairs and other furniture.

"My room," she whispered. The two windows had drawn blinds and curtains. Zack moved to one of the windows, parted the curtains and knelt, raising the blind enough for vision. The room overlooked the greater part of Railroad Street. Alongside the Good Time was an open lot, studded with hitch racks for the use of patrons on busy nights.

Except for a dozen or so pedestrians and a few pieces of wheeled equipment, Railroad Street seemed normally inactive and drab at this breakfast hour. But Zack saw the shadow of the man Noah had spotted lurking beneath the water tank on the roof of Traveler's Rest which stood on the opposite side of the hitch lot. He could see only the front of the livery barn beyond the hotel, and had only a slanting view of the big window in the loft which faced on Railroad Street.

He flipped open the cylinder on Gussie's small gun. There was only one live shell left in the weapon. Gussie saw his grimace. "I'll fix that," she said and hurriedly left the room.

Zack kept watch on the street. The marshal's office and quarters were in sight beyond the livery yard, for the street meandered eastward in stride with the railroad track. The marshal had his living quarters at the rear of the office, for Zack had glimpsed into those rooms the morning he had been assessed a fine by the judge.

Gussie returned, closing the door behind her as silently as possible. She carried a holstered pistol—a .44 that looked well-kept and efficient.

"I know where Mel Lang, the night trouble-shooter, hides his artillery when he's off duty," she said.

Zack buckled on the belt, made sure the gun was loaded. Anita, who had taken his place at the lookout, spoke. "Riders coming in."

Zack crouched beside her. Three horsemen were entering town. One was The Ax. With him were the Ogallala Kid and Matt Pecos.

The Ax was warily scanning the street as he rode closer. He particularly appraised the marshal's office and apparently decided that Hickok had not yet appeared.

The Ax located the gunman on the hotel roof, and peered toward the livery barn, evidently having received a signal. He did not look again, but his attitude was of approval and satisfaction. The trap had been set. Set by Frank Niles, beyond a doubt.

The three men turned into the hitch lot almost below the window from which Zack and Anita were peering, dismounted from their jaded horses and walked tiredly into the honky-tonk. Their footsteps came up from below, indicating that they had gone to the bar and were ordering drinks.

Zack returned to his lookout point, with Anita crouching at his side. It was her quick eyes that saw the movement first.

"Hickok!" she breathed.

The gun marshal had stepped from the door of his office.

Chapter 12

Wild Bill Hickok was immaculately garbed, as always. He wore his spotless Panama hat, a white shirt and dark, thin tie, with black sleeve supporters and tailored dark trousers tucked into expensive, hand-tooled boots. He wore his brace of six-shooters. They had polished cedar handles with silver mountings.

Zack saw the shadow beneath the water tank on the hotel roof come to life. Zack lifted the blind higher and pushed up the lower sash of the window. The gunman, whose name was Buck Anders, according to Noah, was now creeping toward the front parapet of the flat-roofed hotel building. He had two six-shooters in his hands. He crouched there, waiting for his prey to come within certain range, lifting his head occasionally for quick glimpses.

Zack saw a head appear from the loft window of the livery. That assassin was closer to Hickok and was almost sure to fire at any moment.

The man on the roof arose also, lifting one of his six-shooters and taking aim.

Zack shouted, "It's a trap, Hickok! Duck!"

He fired at the man on the roof as he spoke. His bullet struck home. The impact sent the man twisting and reeling backward, his fingers convulsively tripped the hammer of his weapon but the bullet only blew a cloud of dust in the street yards from the marshal. Then he toppled backward from the roof and landed on the wooden awning that shaded the office and lobby. He lay there twisting in the agony of violent death. His pistol lay beside him.

Hickok had crouched and leaped aside. He stared up, locating Zack by the powder smoke that spun into the bright sunlight. His six-shooters were in his hands, the hammers tilted back.

"The hayloft!" Zack yelled. "Look out! There may be others! Take cover!"

A gun opened up from the livery hayloft, but the assassin evidently had been rattled by the shooting, and he was firing fast and wildly. Hickok was not hit. The marshal's two guns answered in split-second reply to that attack. Evidently he had his target in sight, for the weapon in the loft went silent.

Hickok remained crouching for a space, his guns swinging from side to side like the heads of serpents as he conned the street for more opponents.

"Take cover, I tell you!" Zack shouted. "There are three more of them, at least, in the bar. The Ax is one of them."

Hickok did not take cover. Instead, he arose and began running directly toward the Good Time, his guns gripped for battle. He was following the hard code he had learned that attack was always the best defense.

Zack heard the stampede of running feet and the slam of the rear door being thrown open. More running feet in the rear of the building. The Ax and his companions had chosen to escape rather than face Hickok in a gun duel.

Girls were screaming in the rooms. Anita screamed also, but, for her, it was the set expression on Zack's face at which she stared in fear. He turned to leave the room, but she darted in front of him, trying to stop him.

"No!" she sobbed. "No. Please! There are too many of them."

He kissed her. "This has got to be settled now and once for all," he said. "We both know that we could never live in peace with ourselves again if we let Niles get away now that we have him on the run."

She sagged a little, but stood aside. "I'll wait," she choked.

Zack raced to the stairs, descended and pushed open the door to the main room. "It's me, Zack Keech!" he shouted. "Hold your fire, Marshal. They've pulled out. They're likely joining up with Niles at the railroad station."

Wild Bill had entered by way of the swing doors at the front and was standing aside, against a wall, his guns ready to kill. The few patrons were cowering under cover of upended poker tables. The bartender was not visible back of his customary barrier.

"The Tollivers are upstairs," Zack said quickly. "With Gussie Bluebell. She saved all our lives. Frank Niles is ramrod of the highbinders. He kidnapped the Tollivers, forced them to sign an order to sell the Rocky at bankruptcy prices, then tried to murder them and me and all other witnesses who could tell the truth—including you."

Hickok was staring at him. "My God, Keech!" he exclaimed. "What have they done to you?"

He was seeing Zack's injuries—the matted, dried blood, the bruises, the ugly blotches of cigar burns.

"Never mind that," Zack said. "We've got to find Niles and finish this before he can organize for a stand."

Hickok studied him. "How many?"

"I can't say," Zack said. "The Ax, the Ogallala Kid, Matt Pecos, at least. Maybe others, but my bet is that the bulk of them don't really know what this is all about and will fade out. We know for sure there are two less than there were a few minutes ago."

"You better get yourself another gun, at least," Hickok said. "And full loads in that one you have. That will still make only the two of us against stiff odds."

"Make it three of us," the deep voice of Noah Washburn spoke. He stepped into the room by way of the back door. He had his shotgun in his hands. "I got myself some buckshot shells at the store," he added. "Traded in a bushel o' turnips. I've been tormented an' robbed by them whelps, an' it's time everybody in this town stood up to be counted an' help make this country fit for honest people to live in."

Another voice spoke. "I don't aim to miss this party either. I've been pushed around by these thugs. They wrecked my train once. Killed my fireman. I'm in this too."

The speaker was a big man who had emerged from back of an upended table. "I thought it was a private fight, but it seems anybody can pitch in," he added. He was the rawboned, redheaded engineer, Stan Durkin, who had been the victim of Zack's knockout punches on two occasions.

Durkin looked at Zack. "I ain't sayin' I was right in stampedin' your cattle that day," he said. "I ain't sayin' I was wrong. Nor I ain't sayin' you're a better man than me, even if you did level me twice. But I don't run with outlaws or thieves. I got scores of my own to settle with some folks."

Another man moved in. "Count me in," he said. "There'll likely be others as soon as the word spreads. We ain't lettin' you two go ag'in odds like that. We've been pushed around by these scum long enough."

The speaker was the grizzled buffalo hunter, Ed Hake, who had punctured the water tank on the roof of the Good Time with a bullet the day Zack had arrived in Sioux Wells. He was carrying his heavy buffalo rifle and had a six-shooter in his belt.

Hickok looked at the army that had suddenly sprung up. "Noah," he said gently. "You've got a family to support. Stay out of this."

"Nope," Noah said. "There's a time when a man's got to stand up for hisself. Mattie kin git along if anythin' happens to me."

"Of course, of course," Hickok said. He eyed Stan Durkin. "I don't see any gun on you. What are you goin' to use, rocks?"

Durkin clenched his fists, poised them and laughed. "I ain't exactly unarmed. I'll get more satisfaction usin' these."

The barkeeper had emerged from hiding. Zack spoke to him. "You've got artillery back there, hidden. Pass it over, along with any shells you can rake up."

The bartender hurriedly produced from various hiding points, two six-shooters and a sawed shotgun. Zack thrust one of the pistols in his belt after making sure it and the gun he already had were loaded. He offered the shotgun to Stan Durkin, but Durkin refused it. However, reluctantly, he did accept the other six-shooter.

"Come on!" Zack said, and led the way out of the Good Time.

"I could round up a few more of the boys," Durkin said. "A lot of us railroaders have scores to settle with these thugs."

"No time," Hickok said. "Time's one thing we can't afford. We've got to hit them now, and fast. Likely they'll run."

"The Ax won't run," Zack said. "I've had experience with him."

"That's his choice," Hickok said.

He and Zack walked side-by-side down the sidewalk, with Noah and Stan Durkin and the buffalo hunter following. They kept to the shade of the balconies and wooden awnings, then right-wheeled and crossed the unpaved street toward the railroad station.

The station was silent, standing stark and ugly in its red paint, flanked by its plank sidewalk and the steel rails and the greasy ties, all beginning to simmer in the hot sun. The baggage truck stood untended, no clatter came from the telegraph sounders. There was no sign of life in the ticket booth.

A head appeared at a window in the offices above. It was that of Frank Niles. He was hatless, unshaven, and even in that glimpse Zack saw the man's desperation, his bitterness. Niles had six-shooters in his hands.

"You! You!" he shouted, as though he could think of no greater expression of hatred. He fired at Zack, not Hickok, as though that was the epitome of his plight.

But Zack was moving, ducking aside and the shots missed. He fired one pistol in return, but his shot was only an echo to the roar of Hickok's guns, so swiftly had the marshal replied to Niles' murder try.

But Niles had vanished from the window in time and Hickok's bullets only shattered glass. The other guns opened up from hiding places. One outlaw was in the baggage room, firing through its wide open door from its interior gloom. Gunflame spurted from the slit in a partly opened door of a boxcar sitting on a nearby sidetrack.

All the guns were now roaring. Zack and his contingent were scattering. He heard the boom of Noah's shotgun, saw splinters fly from the door of the boxcar. Hickok was running—straight ahead, carrying the fight to his opponent. Zack ran with him stride for stride, but Hickok's objective was the gunman in the baggage room. The marshal fired one gun and Zack glimpsed a figure reeling and crumbling in the baggage room. Matt Pecos.

Zack ran into the waiting room of the station and headed for the stairs and Frank Niles. And The Ax if he was up there.

He heard the deafening roar of guns back of him, saw glass and splinters fly from the ticket booth as it was shot full of holes by Ed Hake. An outlaw had been crouching out of sight below the counter, and the buffalo hunter had sent slugs smashing through wood to find him.

Gunfire had resumed from the boxcar. Noah Washburn

was busy reloading, but Stan Durkin raced across the track, fired twice through the slitted door into the car, then slammed the door and bolted it.

Zack mounted the stairs three steps at a time. As his head and shoulders cleared the upper floor The Ax appeared in the door of one of the offices, firing two guns. But he was dying as he pulled the triggers, for Zack had sent slugs through his stomach the instant he had appeared. The Ax toppled back into the office.

Zack ran to that door. Frank Niles was there, cornered. He began firing as Zack appeared. Zack felt the harsh drive of a slug along his side. Then he sent two bullets into Niles' body. He stepped over The Ax's writhing body, to deliver the death blow to Niles, but found that he could not pull the triggers again. It was not in him to put more bullets in a dying man.

Hickok arrived and ran down the corridor, kicking doors open. He fired into one room and a man gasped, "Don't shoot again, Hickok. I'm hit bad."

Zack, guns ready to back up the marshal, moved to that door. The Ogallala Kid lay there clutching at his stomach. "I'm done for," the Kid gasped. And he was right.

Two more outlaws, hands raised, came from hiding. "My God, Hickok!" one of them chattered, looking at the crumpled bodies. "You've got a charmed life."

Zack sat down, used the remnants of his shirt which still clung to his belt to stem the flow of blood from the wound in his side. He decided it was only an ugly flesh wound. The slug had glanced along a rib.

Frank Niles was still alive, but going fast. Zack stood over him. "That paper you forced the Tollivers to sign," he said harshly. "It won't do you any good now. Where is it?"

Niles managed a ghastly smile. "Go to hell," he said.

"None of this would have happened if you hadn't come to Sioux Wells."

Niles never spoke again. But the papers were still there. Zack found them in Niles' desk, ready to be taken east to Niles' brother. That was late in the day after the dead had been placed in a temporary morgue in Tim Sullivan's livery barn and the prisoners locked in the town jail.

That was after Gussie Bluebell had made a spectacle of herself by kissing and weeping over Hickok and Ed Hake and Noah Washburn and Stan Durkin, none of whom had suffered more than bullet burns.

That was after Julia Tolliver and her granddaughter had also made spectacles of themselves by kissing these same persons and by wailing over Zack as though he was dying, even though he kept trying to reassure them that it wasn't more than a scratch. And there was Anita babbling about how much she loved him, and how she didn't want to live if he died. It was all loud and unruly.

That was after half the citizens of Sioux Wells, sworn in as possemen, had headed out to Box Springs Ranch to clean out the last of the highbinders with plans for stringing up some they considered were likely candidates.

They started straggling back long after nightfall, somewhat disappointed, for they found Box Springs Ranch mainly deserted. The word had reached the hangout in time and the only person they brought back with them was Lila. She had been tied to a post and left to be caught by desperadoes whom she had browbeaten and scorned.

They brought back the first installment of the rich store of loot they found in the caches, but the biggest haul was the gold dust that had been taken from a Rocky express car not long in the past.

"Looks like we'll soon be able to start buildin' on west to the mines," Julia crowed exultantly.

It was a month later when Brandy Ben Keech and his K-Bar-K crew, who were on their way back to Texas, rode within sight of Sioux Wells. Zack led a welcoming party on horseback out to escort them. Fall was crisp in the air. The last of the leaves from the cottonwoods were blowing in the wind. Sioux Wells was beginning to button up for winter.

Zack dismounted and gripped hands with his father, and the crew. "Welcome to Sioux Wells," he said.

Brandy Ben was staring at Zack's companions. He was answering his son's questions numbly, still staring. "Yeah," he mumbled. "We sold the herd. Beat the deadline. Got your telegram at North Platte that you was hangin' out at this place, so we headed this way. Say, that's a mighty purty gal there with you. Never saw purtier dark eyes. An' ain't that feller with the long mustache Wild Bill Hickok?"

"Sure is," Zack said. "And you're right about the young lady being rather pretty. But watch out for her. She stomps on you when she's riled. Packs a derringer at times too. Fact is, she sort of used stomping and a derringer to rope me into marrying her."

"Marryin'?"

"We've been holding off on the ceremony until you and the boys show up. It's to be held tonight in the Good Time, an establishment which is now owned by a fine lady they call Gussie Bluebell. She's furnishing all the refreshment. Wait until you meet my future ma-in-law. She's something. She and Anita here own the Rocky Mountain Express railroad."

"Railroad?" Brandy Bill stuttered. "Say, as I recall it, you went stampedin' off to this town to collect—"

"We'll discuss that later," Zack said. "There's much to be said on both sides."

"He's our division superindendent," Anita explained. "I'm sure you'll get a square deal from him, but the Rocky isn't in shape right now to throw money around recklessly. Isn't that so, Zachary?"

"Well I'll be double-da—danged!" Brandy Ben gasped. He started to hurl his hat on the ground, then thought better of it, for he had paid thirty dollars for it at Miles City.

He looked at Hickok. "You the law here?" he asked.

"Not any longer," Hickok said. "Feller named Stan Durkin is marshal now. I might ride along south with you boys as far as Dodge an' might winter there. Next year I'm of a mind to take a peek at the Dakota country. I hear there's a lot of action at a gold camp named Deadwood up that way."

GLADSTONE CITY LIBRARY

Cliff Farrell was born in Zanesville, Ohio, where earlier Zane Grey had been born. Following graduation from high school, Farrell became a newspaper reporter. Over the next decade he worked his way west by means of a string of newspaper jobs and for thirty-one years was employed, mostly as sports editor, for the *Los Angeles Examiner*. He would later claim that he began writing for pulp magazines because he grew bored with journalism. His first Western stories were written for *Cowboy Stories* in 1926 and his byline was A. Clifford Farrell. By 1928 this byline was abbreviated to Cliff Farrell, and this it remained for the rest of his career. In 1933 Farrell was invited to contribute a story for the first issue of *Dime Western*. He soon became a regular contributor to this magazine and to *Star Western* as well. In fact, many months he would have a short novel in both magazines. Farrell became such a staple at Popular Publications that by the end of the 1930s he was contributing as much as 400,000 words a year to their various Western magazines. In all, Farrell wrote nearly 600 stories for the magazine market. His earliest Western fiction tended to stress action and gun play, but increasingly his stories began to focus on characters in historical situations and the problems faced by those characters. *Follow the New Grass* (1954) was Farrell's first Western novel, a story concerned with a desperate battle over grazing rights in the Cheyenne Indian reserve. It was followed by *West with the Missouri* (1955), an exciting story of riverboats, gamblers, and gunmen. *Fort Deception* (1960), *Ride the Wild Country* (1963), *The Renegade* (1970), and *The Devil's Playground* (1976) are among the best of Farrell's later Western novels. *Desperate Journey*, a first collection of Cliff Farrell's Western short stories, has also been published.